I0571821

The Start of Something Good

Jamett & Joseph Series, Book One

Renee Vincent

writing as
Gracie Lee Rose

THE START OF SOMETHING GOOD
Copyright © 2012, Renee Vincent writing as Gracie Lee Rose
Digital ISBN: 978-0-98558-311-8
Trade Paperback ISBN: 978-0-98558-310-1

Cover Art Design: Renee Vincent
Editors: Wendy Williams and Karen Block

For God,
Who brought happiness back into my life through the goodness and warmth of others. Thank you for the many blessings you've given me.

For Madeline,
Your beautiful smile and genuine sincerity continue to brighten my entire world. I look at how you treat those around you and swell with pride. I'm honored to call you my daughter. I love you, sweetheart.

For Jolee,
Your infectious laughter, bear-tight hugs, and sarcastic sense of humor are truly the best. You have given me so many reasons to smile. I love you always.

THE START OF SOMETHING GOOD

Who knew Mr. Right lived right next door?

Jamie Sutherland, coffee shop owner and serial ruined-relationship survivor, moves into a beautiful loft apartment for a change of scenery. What she doesn't plan on getting is an eye-full of her handsome next-door neighbor—in nothing but a towel—arguing with his significant other in the hallway.

Joseph Scarbrough's world crashes down on him one cruel morning when his childhood sweetheart rips his heart out of his chest and walks away. His humiliation isn't complete until he turns around to pick up the pieces and sees a beautiful brunette who just witnessed his Dear John moment.

Caught in an awkward situation, the two backpedal into their separate worlds. But fate seems determined to make their worlds collide on a regular basis. Is it destiny just being clumsy when it comes to the two unlikely neighbors or is it the start of something good?

Chapter One

"You're such a jerk!"

The malicious tone and volume of a woman's complaint caused my head to turn in the direction of the chaos a few doors down the hall of my apartment complex. After whipping her scarf around her neck in finality, the angered woman marched down the corridor. A man, who I assume was the jerk in question, pursued her. At this moment, I realized their argument was not meant for my eyes or ears. The guy showed up for the fight in nothing but a towel. His bare chest and arms boasted the remnants of a golden summer tan, even in late November.

I rolled my eyes. How was it possible that men still looked divine in winter, while we women have to make an occasional visit to the tanning salon so we don't appear pasty white? Sure, some of us tried rockin' the pale skin look of the Twilight vampire craze, but it never seemed to catch on with the male population. They still preferred their women toned and tanned. Realize, this was merely my conclusion given no man had yet to fall head over heels for me.

"How can I be a jerk for trying to help you forget about your horrible day?" he asked, grasping the woman's arm and tugging her back. Thankfully, he was oblivious to me standing three doors down.

"No, you're a jerk because *you* tried to forget about *my* horrible day by coming on to me," the girl corrected.

The woman then looked past the man's shoulders and suddenly took notice of my presence. The minute our eyes met, heat flushed my entire body. I quickly averted my attention and pretended not to notice their public tiff, fiddling with my keys to find the right one for locking up. I didn't know what angered her more—the fact that I had taken an interest in their argument or that I had seen her boyfriend in a state of near nakedness.

I half expected her to call me out. Instead, she went back to berating the guy. From where I stood, I had established him as a normal, sexually-active (given he came on to her), heterosexual male. It also bears mentioning that he looked very fine in his bathroom apparel.

"I came to you because I needed you, Joseph."

Ah, the jerk in the towel had a name. Not sure why I made a mental note of it, but I did.

"And I'm still here," he concluded, spreading his arms wide. "You're the one who's leaving."

Clearly, the man was not in tune with the proverbial

emotional needs of modern day women. If I were keeping score, he'd have lost a point for that little sarcastic remark. However, his choice of morning attire kept the tally in his favor.

"You just don't get it, do you?" she barked back, slamming her hands upon her hips. "You think everything can be solved with a song or sex."

A song? Now this just got a little more interesting.

"You didn't like what I wrote?" he asked.

With my eyes still buried in the ring of keys clutched in my gloved hands, I couldn't help but notice the slight hint of sadness in Joseph's voice. My heart longed to sneak a peek at him, another potential point in his favor should I see a pitiful expression of pain in his face. But the girl's harsh reaction forbade me to even try a nonchalant glance his way.

"Oh, don't you dare! Don't you dare turn this around and make me the bad guy."

Okay, I was weak. I couldn't help it. I had to catch a glimpse of what was to come. I inserted the correct key into the lock of my apartment door and peered out of the corner of my eye. She poked him in the chest. Repeatedly.

"Again, this is why you are a jerk. You think the world revolves around you and that you play no part in its destruction when it's crumbling around you. You're above it all, yet so far up its ass you can't see the light of day."

He didn't budge or even stop her finger-poke punishment. He stared at her, stunned. "I can't believe you didn't like the song. I was up all night. I wrote that for *you,* Caroline."

My eyes grew wide of their own volition. A songwriter? My sexy, half-dressed, James Tudor underwear model-like neighbor was a songwriter? My heart melted as I stood there. I imagined this man—yes...he was still sporting the towel—hunkered down over a well-worn set of piano keys, pounding out words of love and emotion with each lyrical stanza, every consecutive note inspired by the last. In my mind, I stood tall and proud, holding a white square sign with a bold, black, number ten on it above my head. Fireworks went off behind me in the distance, and a fluttering cloud of confetti fell around me.

This guy is a keeper!

I wanted to run up and give him a congratulatory hug on his big win, but the girlfriend—or soon-to-be-ex-girlfriend, if all of my assumptions were on the money—rolled her eyes and turned her back to him.

"You were never cut out to be a songwriter, Joseph. Just like you, your music lacks heart."

She left him standing in the narrow hallway, injured and bleeding. The knife in his chest remained at such a vicious angle that I began to wonder if he'd ever live through it. If it were me, I would have been crushed to the core. Then again, I wouldn't have settled for someone like her. I would have been smart enough to keep my standards raised and my heart better guarded.

Inwardly, I sighed. I supposed it was easier for me to say those things when I was outside looking in. I shouldn't have been listening in the first place. That's when my brain kicked into panic overdrive.

If he turned around right now, he'd see that I'd partaken in being a rude onlooker with a front row seat to his pathetic break-up. And I'd no longer be the cute, little neighbor who he—hypothetically speaking—might run into one day because he wasn't watching where he was going as he walked down the hall. He wouldn't suddenly feel compelled to ask me out on a date because he was a hopeless romantic and believed wholeheartedly in love at first sight. And fate. Surely fate had a part in all this.

My mind raced as I continued to stand there like a deer in headlights, freaking out over the moment when he'd give up staring down the hall and turn toward his door. If I made a break for the elevator, he'd see me do so. If I stayed where I was, he'd still see me. No matter what I decided, I was doomed to be caught eavesdropping.

Considering the perilous situation I was in, one would

think I wouldn't dare take one more peek down the hall. But I did.

My terrycloth-kilted neighbor ran frustrated fingers through his dark, nigh-in-need-of-a-cut hair and, just as I feared, turned around.

I don't know who was more shocked, him or me. It was evident he hadn't expected to see anyone in the hall, much less a pale, brunette with barely a curve to her body, all of which were hidden behind a fluffy winter parka, scarf, and gloves.

I stared, frozen in my boots, my eyes bulging from their sockets. He returned the same stunned look. For a split second, I thought I saw the corners of his mouth twitch upward in a smile. So, I smiled back out of courtesy.

Short-lived as that thought was, his brow furrowed. He glanced back over his shoulder as if gathering his bearings on where he and his girlfriend had chosen to have their dispute and determining whether it were possible I witnessed it all from where I stood. I could have sworn I saw a hint of embarrassment on his face as he scratched his head. "Did you…I mean, did we disturb you? Could you actually hear us from inside?"

"Oh, no," I tried to explain at the same time I aimed to comfort him. "You didn't disturb me. I was out here the whole time." I clamped my mouth shut. I had just blatantly admitted to eavesdropping on his personal conversation.

He eyes widened, and his chin tilted upward a bit. "Really…"

"I-I mean, not the whole time, just…well…."

It was my turn to be embarrassed, and I squeezed my eyes closed. Tightly. At least now, I could proudly say I was both weak and a horrible conversationalist.

Okay, you big idiot, say goodbye, cut your losses, and consider yourself lucky that he doesn't know your name. For all he knows, you're just a friend of the person who lives in Loft B and you were just leaving.

Better yet, perhaps he'll be so distraught over this whole morning that days from now when he runs into you again, as you're visiting your friend in Loft B, he won't even recognize you.

I liked the idea. So much that I'd already started plotting out my strategy. I'd donate this coat and the rest of my winter outerwear to Goodwill and buy a whole new ensemble, just in case he had a photographic memory. I'd act like we had never met and start anew.

He came closer, his eyes zeroing in on me. They rivaled the bluest Montana sky on a summer afternoon. "You're the new girl, right? You just moved in a couple weeks ago. Sutherland, is it?"

There went that plan. Wait. Did he just reveal in a very subtle, yet sly fashion that he took enough notice of me to remember my name? And *how* did he know my name? Had he broken into my mailbox and rummaged through my mail? Or worse, the dumpster?

No. I refused to believe this beautiful creature, as bold as he was talking to me in a towel, would resort to dumpster diving for any reason. Still, the question remained.

"Yeah, that's me. I'm Sutherland. Jamie Sutherland."

I had to look away. Joseph's eyes threatened to spellbind me, and I wondered how Caroline had the strength to deflect his hypnotic powers. By the looks of her glamorous appeal, I imagined she was a regular temptress herself, with the ability to stop traffic a mile away. I, on the other hand, was a plain Jane; brown hair, brown eyes, small build without a voluptuous curve in sight—the girl next door with the body of a twelve-year old boy—which was how a grudge-nursing ex-boyfriend once described me four years ago. To this day, I still choke up over his unpleasant portrayal.

"Welcome to the building, Jamie."

I dared to sneak another peek at him, hoping I could get through this conversation without looking like a faint-hearted schoolgirl. "How did you know my name?" I finally asked.

"Your name is on the mailbox for Loft B. I just put

two and two together and came up with you."

It was nice to know the man knew his math. It should come in handy when he counted the reasons why he should've steered clear of me. Granted, I was not as needy as that Caroline girl, nor was I an attention-seeking drama queen. I avoided sinking to those emotional levels at all costs. I was a strong, independent woman who had no need for a man in her life. I'd tried the "couple" thing—multiple times—and I'd failed royally each go round.

Given the copious amounts of money I'd lost and the countless tears I'd shed over those "Mr. Rights" gone horribly wrong, I swore never to get sucked into the ridiculous notion of romance and all the frilly fringe benefits that supposedly came with it. I was a pessimistic woman. What I remembered most about love was not the endearing looks, warm hugs, or the cute butterflies in the stomach. It was the sucker punch in the gut when I least expected it.

"I should go," I said in haste, trying to remind myself that even this Greek Adonis-like man with kind blue eyes was capable of throwing a TKO punch.

He grinned, glanced down at his rather inappropriate attire, and thumbed over his shoulder toward his open apartment door. "Me too. Gotta get to work."

The innocence in his smile knocked me off balance.

He went from bold and witty to downright adorable. It was a good thing he had already started to take a few steps backward, else I might have reached out and pinched his cute, five-o'clock-shadowed cheeks. The longer I stood here, the more I was convinced Caroline was clinically insane for going all diva on this man.

Stepping beneath his doorframe, he nodded once, reaffirming the beauty of his boyish grin, and closed the door.

A breath I had no idea I was even holding escaped me. My arms fell limp at my sides, keys rattling in my hand. I still had no grasp of what had really happened. The only thing that registered was Joseph and how he was quite possibly the best-looking jerk I'd ever seen.

Chapter Two

All the way to work, I recapped the morning.

Joseph was a healthy, heterosexual male, a songwriter, who had a steady job, or at least, I assumed he had one since he said he had to get to work—wherever that might be. He was not afraid to express his emotions, though he may have some issues with understanding and predicting the emotions of the opposite sex. A major setback as far as the female race was concerned, but I could work on that. It was fixable with the right amount of nurturing.

He was confident, bold—without the arrogance—and looked mighty fine after a shower. His eyes were blue, his lashes long, and his face chiseled. His hair hung in his face at times, but not enough to annoy me. In fact, it had taken everything I had not to thread my eager fingers through its wild softness. And the best part of all—after checking his left hand for a ring or a tell-tale tan line—Caroline was indeed just a girlfriend and not a wife.

Three hours into work, and I was still thinking of this guy. I had more pressing things to do than wonder whether

I'd run into him again when I got home, like unpacking the rest of my things from my recent move. Although I wouldn't really call it a move, since I was still in the same area code as before. I'd left one apartment complex, for reasons too boring to mention, and moved into another a few blocks away.

I didn't care much for drastic changes, and I was not a wanderer. I enjoyed knowing I'd lived in the Northern Kentucky/Southern Ohio area all my life. In the last seven years of it, I owned my own little coffee shop in downtown Cincinnati called *I Like You a Latte*. It might sound like a spin-off *Starbucks*, but my little corner café offers great tasting coffee without the hefty prices.

"Can I get you anything else?" I asked routinely, before cashing the customer out. While I ran on autopilot for most of the day, my brain continued to take detours toward Destination Joseph. The view was always great, but the amount of time I spent in this one-track automobile was getting to me.

"You okay?"

I glanced in the direction of the voice and smiled. Melissa knew me better than I sometimes knew myself. I had hired her the same day she applied, assuming she would be the perfect person to help me take this pipe dream and turn it into a successful business venture. As I'd thought, she was all that and more. Melissa was not only a great employee, but also a wonderful, loyal friend.

"I'm fine," I played off, wiping spilled cream from the counter in front of the espresso machine.

Melissa stacked more cups beside the countless flavored elixir bottles. "You seem frazzled."

I wanted to laugh. Joseph had caused me to feel a lot of emotions in such a short time today, but frazzled was not one of them. I went for slightly off-kilter. "Thanks for asking, but really, I'm fine."

"Does he have a name?"

Joseph almost left my mouth before I caught on to her sly inquiry. I held my tongue and rolled my eyes. "There is no *he*. Therefore, there is no name to speak of. Good try."

Melissa gave my hip a disco bump and continued arranging the lids. "He's *that* good looking, huh?"

"I don't know what you're talking about." I tried to sound convincing, but again, I sucked at lying. The look on Melissa's face illustrated that very point. "Look," I placated, aiming for a different approach. "I just had a rough start this morning. I was up late unpacking—"

"Still?" Melissa interrupted. "I thought you said it would only take a few days."

"Yes, it would if I were in the mood to rummage through boxes of stuff I probably don't need. I already unpacked the essentials."

"So, get rid of the extra boxes. Toss them. Don't even look inside. If you haven't needed anything from them in the past two weeks, you probably can do without them altogether."

Melissa's logic sounded perfectly rational. I'd love to be able to chuck the unpacked boxes of crap and never look back. The problem was I inherited the pack rat gene. I couldn't get rid of anything. For whatever reason, I looked at my junk, even items of fad clothing and college memorabilia from fifteen years ago, and couldn't get away from this crazy idea I'd need it someday. My inability to declutter was a curse.

"I told you I'd help you," Melissa reminded me. "We could get it finished in one night."

Somehow I doubted that. Melissa, as good a friend as she was, had never seen my 'stash,' and I'd rather keep it that way. "I appreciate the offer, but I'll get it done one of these nights."

"Well, you better do it fast before this cute guy asks you out." Melissa leaned in close and spoke softly so only I could hear. "Nothing's worse than being in the middle of a hot, toe-curling kiss at the door, and you can't invite him in because there are boxes on every flat surface in your apartment." She raised her brow, hoping I caught the subtle hint.

I slapped my wet rag at her and frowned. Her attempts to get me to admit there was a man in my life were ridiculous. Joseph was not in my life. He was in my apartment building on the same floor, but nothing more. I'd hardly call our encounter in the hallway this morning an introduction to a love affair. If that were the case, I'd be having a seriously torrid affair with the teenaged dog walker who insisted on holding the lobby door open for me each evening so I could trip over five drooling hounds on tangled leashes.

"For the last time," I said, my voice taking on a strange tone of seriousness and determination. "There is no one in my life, nor is he about to ask me out. I barely know him."

"I knew it!" Melissa fist-pumped triumphantly.

Most everyone in the joint looked in my direction. I closed my eyes and hung my head.

Ignoring the weight of our customers' stares, Melissa slid closer to me. "How did you two meet? Come on, you can tell me. Is he that construction worker who whistled at you the other day from the scaffold across from *The Red Squirrel?*"

I cringed. I remembered that guy, and I wanted to elbow Melissa hard for even bringing his foul image into my head. "Eww…no."

Another idea popped into her head. Her eyes grew wide, and she almost started jumping up and down. Melissa was always an animated chatterbox. "Is he the professor from NKU who asked for directions to the Aronoff Art Center after he bought a Pumpkin Spice Latte, light on the cream, double cinnamon?"

"No, he is not. And how in the world do you remember what the professor ordered?" If I recalled correctly, he came in almost three weeks ago and hadn't been back since.

Melissa rubbed her neck nervously as if she'd suddenly developed chickenpox. "I don't know how I remember those things. But I'm glad your man is not the professor." She bit her lip. "'Cause I was hoping to get all over that the next time he comes in."

I was not surprised. Melissa always had a thing for male teachers.

"Come on, Jamett Penelope Sutherland, tell me who he is."

I glanced around, hoping no one had heard her. I gave her a strict look. "You know you're not supposed to call me by my full name. *No one* is allowed to call me that, not even my own mother who blessed me with that horrible name."

"Tell me his name, and yours shall remain…" She made a zipping-of-the-lips gesture and baited me with challenging eyes.

I knew Melissa wouldn't share my despicable secret in this blackmailing fashion, but the look on her face had me second-guessing. "I only know his first name," I confessed.

"A first name will do," she reasoned. "I can tell a lot from a man's first name."

I cocked my brow. "Like what?"

"Like if he's upstanding and intelligent versus a dimwitted louse. You know what I mean. Never will you find a man with the name of Maxwell to be an unemployed drug addict. He'd be wealthy and well mannered, unlike Willard or Clyde. You can just see the picket fence of rotten teeth and smell the stench of day-old cigarettes and Jack Daniels with those names."

"Oh my goodness," I feigned my best look of disgust and disappointment. I swallowed hard, hard enough that Melissa could see my throat bob. "His name is Clyde."

I loved the look on her face. It was priceless. Immediately, she began comforting me by rubbing my arms and adjusting her own explanation. "No, I didn't mean Clyde, I meant..." She struggled to come up with a believable name at the drop of a hat. I almost felt sorry for her.

I cracked a smile as she stuttered about, wishing I had a camera so I could capture this moment. It was not every day I could pull one over on Melissa. Eventually, she caught on to my ruse, and it was my turn to be slapped.

"Girl, I oughta…." she warned with a theatrical fist.

I couldn't help but laugh. "His name is Joseph," I surrendered, as I went over to wait on the next customer. From behind me, I could practically hear the gears churning in Melissa's head, turning the name over and over, though I hadn't expected to hear her say it aloud, pairing my name with his.

"Jamett and Joseph."

I flashed a glare over my shoulder, expressing my displeasure of her outspoken thought processes, but she paid it no heed. Instead she mouthed, "I like it," and sashayed her way to the crowded café tables.

Chapter Three

The day had been extra long. I tried to blame it on the fact that it was Friday and the last day of the sale of our seasonal Thanksgiving line of cappuccinos, but rationale told me it was because Joseph had made a lasting impression on my brain. I normally didn't get all hung up on pretty men. Truth be told, I didn't understand what made this guy so special that I'd obsess about him throughout my entire day.

Sure, I had the privilege of eyeing the man in a towel, ogling his tight little gluteus maximus without his knowledge. And I'd salivated over the view of his muscled chest just perfectly dusted with the right amount of hair as he soothed me with the sound of his deep, dulcet voice. But did that really make him worthy of taking root in my thoughts and refusing to leave?

It was kind of rude, if you asked me. I never wanted him there. Towel or no towel.

Okay, that didn't come out right. It was bad enough I had images of this man draped in nothing but soft, white terrycloth, much less introducing thoughts of removing said cloth. Not good.

I shook my head and locked my coffee shop for the night, eager to walk the streets of Cincinnati and breathe the brisk Midwest air without ruminating over Joseph.

I barely took three steps before the man invaded my thoughts again. Seriously? Was I this feeble and weak-minded that I couldn't go a single minute without fanaticizing about Joseph's body and eyes and smile and…

Yeah, I was pathetic.

Accepting myself for the pitiable excuse that I was, I walked the remaining blocks from Fountain Square to the local grocery store on Seventh Street, succumbing to the realization that Joseph, and his exquisite body, would accompany me.

* * * *

After picking up what I needed to fill my pitifully empty refrigerator—and by fill, I meant no more than I could carry on foot without my arms breaking off at the elbows—I entered my apartment complex. Somehow, I dodged the dog walker and made it to the elevator without bumping into a single person who suddenly felt compelled to welcome the new girl.

Upon stepping off, I noticed the hall was clear. No Joseph.

Just as I had this morning, I fumbled with my keys and reminded myself that before I did anything else, I would get rid of any unnecessary ones (yes, I hoard even my keys), so I wouldn't tarry at my door and run the risk of running into Joseph again.

Staying clear of Joseph was pertinent to my sanity. I was trying to forget him.

"Here, let me help you."

I jumped out of my skin at hearing someone's voice behind me. I jerked away so quickly that one of my grocery bags ripped at its bottom, sending a few canned goods to the floor with a thud and several oranges bouncing and rolling down the hall.

Immediately, I bent at the waist to retrieve the nearest oranges before they could get away. This person had the same idea. We hit heads, and I fell flat on my rump. I blinked several times so my eyes could focus. My assaulter had taken off down the hall and, to my surprise, he ran after the unruly fruit.

"I'm sorry. I'm sorry. I'm sorry. I was only trying to help you unlock your door since your hands were full."

I couldn't take my eyes off the man chasing my oranges. It was quite a sight to see. He was dressed in casual slacks, a button-up white shirt, dress shoes, and a tie. When he succeeded in apprehending the fleeing produce, he stood up with his hands above his head, holding the captive goods in a celebratory stance. "Got 'em!"

My eyes nearly popped out of my head. The savior of my rolling oranges was Joseph. I barely recognized him with his clothes on.

I scuffled to my feet, my head pounding, my mind scrambling. This was not supposed to happen. I was *supposed* to get into my apartment, unload my groceries, throw away the useless keys, and collapse in my nice comfy sleigh bed. I had so looked forward to it, and now the opportunity had slipped through my fingers. I felt like I was watching reruns of this morning's reality show. And I hate reality TV.

I grimaced as I gathered myself and my belongings, trying very hard not to look at Joseph. He picked up the ripped brown paper bag and handed it to me with a smile, probably hoping to smooth things other. I didn't return the gesture, hoping he'd kindly back away.

"I truly am sorry. Is your head all right?"

I wanted to push him away. Childish, I know, but he threatened to ruin the balance I'd come to enjoy in my solitary existence.

"Jamie?" He touched my hand, which had begun to

insert the key into the doorknob. My hands were absent gloves this time, and I could feel the warmth of his palm on my wrist. Inwardly, I was thankful that I wore a huge parka, for I had hoped it was thick enough to mute the sound of my hammering heart from his ears.

Our eyes met again, and I swore I lost all feeling in my legs. The spectrum of color in his irises hypnotized me, and I couldn't break the spell.

"Are you all right?" he asked again.

I swallowed and shook off the trance he'd put me in. "Um, yeah." I resumed inserting the key into the lock, despite the pressing realization of his hand still on mine. I turned and pushed, and the door swung open.

Finally, he let go and stepped back.

"Yeah, I'm fine," I tried to smooth over the awkwardness. "I appreciate you chasing my fruit." I held up the one I had in my hand. "Orange you glad you came by when you did?"

He gave a chuckle, though I was certain he only meant to humor me. I was not that funny.

"Actually, I am glad I came by when I did."

I added charming to this guy's list of redeeming qualities. I could've added more if I wanted, but it wouldn't do me a bit of good. I refused to let myself fall for him.

Ignoring his statement and the intensity of his gaze, I

entered my apartment and set the undamaged grocery bag and my purse on the entryway table. When I turned around to salvage the rest of my canned goods from the floor, I froze in my tracks. Joseph was standing in my doorway, holding the oranges as if they were objects of a truce offering, and he branded the most beautiful, honest smile I'd ever seen.

His eyes scanned over my darkened apartment. I wasn't sure what he was looking for, but I knew I wasn't ready for a man to peek into my personal space.

I grabbed the door and closed it enough that only my body could fit through, forcing him to step back into the hall. With my foot, I slid the canned goods past the threshold and confiscated the oranges from his hands.

"I'd love to stick around and chat some more," I fibbed, "but I'm…" I stumbled on my words. *What was I doing tonight?*

"Yeah, me too," he finished for me. "I've got to be somewhere…" He checked his watch, "in an hour. Big date."

Big date, huh? Even I could see he made that up so he didn't look like a pitiful schmuck with nothing to do on a Friday evening because his girlfriend had broken up with him less than twelve hours before.

Two can play this little game.

Before I knew what I was doing, I spilled forth my big imaginary plans for the night. "Yeah, I've got a big date too. He's a professional bodybuilder."

His face furrowed.

Clearly that career choice was not as awe-inspiring for Joseph as it was for me. I needed to do better. "And a doctor. Surgeon. He just does the bodybuilding on the side."

"Really," he nodded, pretending to be moved by my make-believe date's credentials. "Impressive."

"Yeah, he's always so busy, and this is the first night off he's had in months. I'm cooking a huge dinner. Candlelight."

"I see…sounds nice."

I nodded my head in time with his. We seemed to be measuring each other up, hoping to rouse some small amount of jealousy with our sorry stories. Or waiting for the other to give in and initiate the farewells. He broke first.

"Well, I don't want to hold you up."

"Thanks," I replied, starting to close the door. "And thanks again for—"

"No problem," he said, dismissing my gratitude with a wave of his hand. "If not for me, you wouldn't have lost your oranges in the first place."

His sudden change in tone pulled on my heartstrings.

Yes, he was the reason my head hurt and my groceries had hit the floor, but deep down I knew his intentions were good. He was only trying to help me open my door since my hands were full, and I reacted like a skittish rabbit zigzagging in headlights.

If anything, I owed him an apology for the lies I told. Come to think of it, I told so many today that if I were made of wood, I'd put Pinocchio to shame.

Inch by inch, I closed the door. His wave goodbye was the last thing I saw before the lock clicked shut. I listened with my ear pressed against the wood until I heard his footsteps fade down the hall. Only it wasn't his door closing I heard, but the ding of the elevator.

I guess he did have plans. And I was the pathetic schmuck now.

Chapter Four

I could actually say I accomplished something tonight, besides running off the most handsome man in the Midwest. I'd sifted through my keys and thrown away the ones I didn't need. I know it may not sound like a big deal for the average unsentimental person, but for me…it was like parting with ancient family heirlooms.

My key ring now only had six keys on it—one for the security door of the complex, one for my apartment, one for the mailbox, one for the coffee shop, one for my safety deposit box that has nothing in it, and one for the car I used to drive. I didn't own the car anymore, but I loved that automobile. It was a 1989 Chevy Beretta, and it reminded me of the carefree part of myself that rarely came out.

Anyway, I felt good about the forward progress I made at becoming a more efficient, organized woman of the twenty-first century. I could now look around my box-strewn apartment and know that soon the mess and the things connected to me in some way that I longer wanted would all disappear. I felt uplifted and ready to tackle more of the items on my to-do-list. Melissa would be so proud. Funny how a bunch of carved metal trinkets lining the bottom of my trash can could make a person feel like a million bucks.

I was determined not to lose my gumption, so I headed straight for the closest box marked COLLEGE in bold, Sharpie-black letters. I opened the flaps and sighed. The contents inside propelled me back in time. Images of my dorm days and wild frat parties flittered through my mind. An automatic smile creased my lips.

I missed those days when oodles of homework were my chief concern. When my current grade point average, or how to raise it, was my biggest problem. Oh, how I'd take the stresses of the past—like staying up all night trying to finish a six-page report or cramming for an anatomy test—over the stresses of my present career-world.

I reached in and pulled out a stuffed turtle with the symbols Delta Zeta on its shell. This cute little reptile was the mascot of our sorority, and, for whatever reason, I'd felt the need to purchase him from NKU's campus gift shop my freshmen year. He used to sit on my bed next to the pillow my grandmother embroidered for me. I still had that pillow too, though it was already unpacked and sitting on my bed in the next room.

I clenched my teeth together, finding the strength to say goodbye. A woman in her early thirties had no need for a Greek-alphabetized tortoise. Taking a deep breath, I walked over to the garbage can and tossed him on top of the keys.

Hands on my hips, I stared down at the poor little guy. I couldn't do it.

I grabbed the box with COLLEGE written on the side, dumped it out, and set the empty box next to the garbage can. I scratched out COLLEGE and wrote GOODWILL. I reached into the trash and switched him to his new home. While I was still getting rid of the plush reptile, I felt better that I wasn't sending him to a landfill.

With a nod of affirmation, I went back to the heaping pile of college paraphernalia and decided their fates, one by one. Within an hour, I had sifted through the mementos and had moved onto another box labeled CHILDHOOD.

At this point, I decided to open a bottle of wine. My reasons were two-fold. I had successfully eliminated an entire box from my ownership, and I knew this particular one would take more bravado than I had. From my years of co-existing with hunky jocks and cute frat boys on campus, I came to learn that wine was courage in a bottle.

No sooner had I poured and consumed the first gulp of Pinot Grigio, than I heard a loud noise from the hall. It sounded like someone had tripped and fallen. Concerned, I went to my door and peeked out the security hole. I saw nothing.

I knew I hadn't imagined the sound, and because of how loud it was, my curiosity got the better of me. I unlocked the door and peered out. Lying against the wall, in a contorted fashion, was an unconscious Joseph.

I ran to him and dropped to my knees. "Joseph," I called, giving him a little shake. "Joseph, are you okay?"

He stirred and turned his head in my direction, fanning a wisp of alcohol-infused breath in my face. Whiskey. There was no mistaking that smell. The man had not tripped and knocked himself unconscious…he was drunk. So inebriated he was content to sleep wherever his body had fallen.

"Joseph, you need to get up," I lifted his heavy, dead-weighted arms. He stirred again, but made no effort to help me. Instead, he mumbled a chain of slurred words that made no sense. "Yeah, I know, darlin'," I replied, patronizing him. "You've had a rough night."

"Lonely," he managed to say. "'ts lonely night without you."

I assumed his off-the-cuff admittances were meant for Caroline's ears. I couldn't help but pity him. He was a heartbroken man who'd just lost someone he cared for and had no idea how to deal with it. From the looks of him, getting dumped probably wasn't something he was used to. I imagined he'd done his fair share of breaking hearts in his day, but now that the tables were turned, drinking to forget was the only therapy available to him.

Perhaps if I'd have been more compassionate and appreciative after he'd chased my fruit down the hall, he wouldn't have drank himself into an oblivion. As far as he was concerned, two women had shot him down in the same day. For a man of his caliber, I was sure that was a shocker.

Poor guy.

Although…I had to relish this moment. Even in his drunken stupor, he was beautiful. A hunk of dark, unruly hair had fallen over his brow, and nothing stopped me from brushing it back this time. I took in the strong angles of his face, the way the shadow of scruff across his jaw complimented the high rise of his cheekbones. His lips were full and soft. His nose was straight as an arrow. And he had a small dusting of salt at his temples, making him more appealing to my eyes—as if he wasn't already stunning enough.

I was grateful for this moment. I could admire Joseph fully without anyone knowing. Without *him* knowing. Heck, I could probably strip the man of his clothes and get my eye-full and he'd still be none the wiser given his present condition.

As tempting as that sounded, I worried about how I was going to get him into the safety of his apartment. I couldn't just leave him in the hallway all night. And Lord knows I wasn't going to spend the night chaperoning him as he slept in the hall. I needed my sleep too.

With a deep breath and the sudden determination of ten men, I grabbed his wrists and yanked. "Come on, Joseph. On your feet." I pulled for all I was worth, getting a small response from him.

"Wh'ya doin'?" he slurred as his eyes fluttered opened. "'M try'n to sleep."

"Not out here, you're not," I said, pulling harder. "Come on. Let's get you to your bed."

His head teetered on his shoulders, but he seemed to perk up. "Your bed?" he asked with a crooked smile.

"No, *your* bed," I corrected.

"Th-that's what I said," he stuttered, looking at me like I was an idiot.

I decided to go with it. Anything to get this man on his feet and into his apartment where he belonged, so I could get back to mine. "Yeah, Joseph, I'm taking you to your bed."

He cocked his brow, or tried to. The alcohol in his system had numbed even the muscles in his face. He lugged his heavy arm around my shoulders as if he wasn't the slightest bit intoxicated. He made every effort to be suave, but his speech lacked the smooth debonair quality it required to pull it off. "I though' abou' your bed 'll night. An' how I's gonna make y'call m' name."

Again, I assumed the dirty talk was meant for Caroline and not me. If it wasn't so slurred, the idea might have intrigued me. To a degree, my mind wandered with the notion of what Joseph could do to make me call out his name, but of course, it involved the sober version of him, an adaptation that was too far out of reach.

My mind couldn't dwell in that tantalizing picture for long. He staggered so much, even with me trying to support him, that my brain's focus remained on doing everything in my power to keep him upright.

When we finally faced his door, he leaned forward and rested his head on the wall, his legs beginning to buckle.

"Where are your keys?" I asked, jerking him back to a standing position.

I saw a huge grin slice between his lips. "Ther' in m' pocket."

I knew what he expected. But it wasn't going to happen. "Joseph, reach in your pocket and get your keys."

"You do it," he challenged, his face contorting in a weird expression. I assumed it was his best attempt at arousing me with a not-so smoldering stare.

I rolled my eyes and tried to barter with logic. "Joseph, if I get your keys, I'll have to let go of you, and you'll fall. You've got a free hand...use it."

I heard him sigh before he made a move toward his pocket. I was more thankful than ever when he pulled them out and offered them to me. Unfortunately, his key ring looked like mine, that is, the ring of keys I used to have before I discarded the extras. Struggling to hold him up with my left arm, I sifted through the keys until I found a likely candidate. I used my right hand to attempt to unlock his door. I tried many times to get the damn thing to line up in the slot, but with Joseph's body threatening to collapse at my feet, it wasn't an easy task. On the brink of giving up, I finally got the key to engage and kicked the door open.

The sound jolted his head upward, and his eyes flashed open. "Come in!" he shouted, as if awakened by someone knocking. "Door's open!"

I ignored his drunken outburst and led him into his apartment. Grateful for the large windows that ran the length of the wall in our historical building, I silently thanked God for the blessing of the moonlight pouring in so I didn't have to contend with flipping on a lamp. The evening illumination didn't seem to aid Joseph any, however. In fact, it could have been broad daylight and he still would have stumbled into everything in the room.

Needless to say, I was eager to dump his sorry butt in bed and get back to what I was doing. We wandered aimlessly through his living space, with no guidance from my co-pilot, looking for the bedroom. I did, however, find a guitar leaning against the wall. I smiled. Whether he hammered on the ivories or tickled the frets when composing his songs, I couldn't help but hold him in high regard. Drunk or not, I found this man fascinating.

Moving on, I finally located his bedroom. I ushered him into the spacious room and a waft of cologne tickled my senses as we tottered past his dresser. I couldn't name the cologne, but it certainly smelled wonderful. I imagined him coming out of the shower in his towel and splashing some over his damp neck and shoulders.

What are you doing?

Sorry, I was in a man's bedroom. What did you expect from me?

"Joseph," I said, taking a shot at gaining his attention. When he rolled his head in my direction, he looked at me with the most sincere, pleading eyes. I swallowed, trying to disregard how intense they were when his gaze fell over me. "You're safe in your bedroom now. Just lie down."

"Thanks," he mumbled, and collapsed on the mattress.

I assisted him with hoisting his legs up and removing his shoes and tie. Again, weakling that I am, I thought of taking off his shirt, but I couldn't bring myself to do it. Instead, I pulled the thick duvet over his body and smiled down at him.

One last time, I took this moment to marvel at his raw handsomeness. I doubted I would ever get this chance again. We were on different playing fields, and a guy like him would never be interested in a girl like me.

I touched his face with the back of my fingers and lightly stroked his cheek, never thinking he'd feel it. Evidently, he wasn't as numb as I thought. He opened his eyes and stared at me.

"Jamie," I heard him whisper, though his lips barely moved.

I sat on the edge of the bed and leaned closer so I could hear him. "Yeah?"

"She broke m' heart."

Caroline again. Back to Caroline. That woman didn't deserve as much reflection and consideration as she was getting from this man. I tried my best to comfort him. "I know she did. And I'm sorry you had to go through that."

"S'okay now," he mumbled. "Yer here."

His choice of words threw me. They always say drunk men are honest men, but did my simple presence actually bring Joseph comfort? I contemplated the idea a little longer and eventually came to the conclusion I was putting way too much emphasis on a plastered man's inarticulate remarks. Come morning, he'd have no recollection of this night or what he said to me.

I patted his chest—wow, it was solid—and went back to placating him. "Go to sleep, Joseph. It'll all be better in the morning."

"Stay wit' me…"

I froze. No sooner than I heard his words, I felt his hand rest at the small of my back. Through my T-shirt, I felt the heat of his palm and all five pressure points of his fingertips. His touch ignited feelings I had buried long ago. We locked eyes, and for the span of a few breaths, had I been breathing at all, we both seemed to consider the offer.

No.

I blinked rapidly, affirming I was not going to succumb to something as rash, not to mention reckless and utterly foolhardy, as accepting his proposal. The only reason he asked me to stay was because he was brokenhearted, drunk, and desperate. If he were sober and in his right mind, he would never have made such a suggestion in the first place.

No. I will not be the easy, rebound girl.

"Joseph, you don't know what you're saying. Just close your eyes. You never know…Caroline might come to her senses and call you tomorrow."

"I don' wanna see Caroline 'nymore. She doesn' love me. She doesn' look a' me like you do. I like th' way you look a' me."

Surely, I heard wrong. Perhaps it was my overactive imagination running rampant as I lingered in somewhat of a near embrace with this man. My hand remained on the solid wall of his chest, and his hand still pressed against my back. This position hardly had the makings of a lover's clinch, but considering it had been more than two years since I was this close to a man, I deemed our situation as much of an embrace as one could fathom.

It amazed me that Joseph had thought I looked at him in a manner which evoked significance. I remembered hardly making eye contact with him at all, except for those couple of times I fell entranced by his gaze. Like now.

I looked away and pushed myself from him. He caught my wrist and held me affixed to the side of his bed. The strength in his hand startled me, but the sweet, endearing look in his eyes had me melting.

"Thanks."

With one tiny word, he touched my soul. I opened my mouth to speak, but thank goodness the alcohol had begun to take effect on his attention span before I blurted out something I probably would've regretted.

His eyes fluttered, his head relaxed, and his grip released. His arm dropped and hung off the side of the bed. I reached out and placed it gently across his chest, drawing the covers over him. Within a few seconds, he began snoring.

Chapter Five

Mornings were not my favorite time of the day. I was not, nor have I ever been, a morning person. I guess that's why I owned my own coffee shop. I absolutely, positively needed my coffee in the morning to begin to see the goodness in sunlight.

This morning, in particular, was worse than most.

I'd left Joseph's apartment last night with my mind in a whirlwind. It was cluttered with questions, and 'what ifs', and emotions I would've rather not felt. I'd been a single woman, happily living my life without the complications of a man's presence for many years now, and I didn't need this man—albeit a sexy, charming, and extremely intriguing man—to waltz his way in and mess things up,.

I was not one for change. I liked things the way they were, and I didn't feel comfortable getting involved with a guy who was my neighbor. I had searched for just the right place to live near Fountain Square, with all the historical charm and architecture I could afford. When I found this place, I nearly begged on my hands and knees for the owners to approve my application. So, if it didn't work out with Mr. Towel Man, this apartment would no longer be the ideal place to live. It would be awkward and problematic because, although I normally avoided confrontation, I was still a woman with pride.

Today, I was just a grumpy woman with pride who hadn't finished her unpacking last night because a certain gorgeous man put far too many thoughts and images in her mind to work, sleep, or do anything. To make matters worse, my coffee maker was incredibly slow.

I gave it a slap, as if it would make the java juice pour out faster and checked the clock. Nine o'clock. I was determined to rid my apartment of these darn boxes today, if it killed me.

A knock at the door disrupted my internal pep talk. I grumbled and sighed, wondering who in the world it could be. Probably Mrs. Tibbs from Loft A needing another cup of sugar for her baking fetish. She probably assumed I got sugar free since I owned a coffee joint. One of these days I was going to have to break the news to her that I didn't own stock in the sugar cane market. Mentally preparing to do just that, I whipped open the door and gasped.

It was not Mrs. Tibbs, but Joseph, whom I caught trying to smooth his bed-head crop of hair. Immediately, he dropped his arms to his sides and nervously adjusted his stance a few times until he chose a pose where his thumbs jabbed in the front of his jean pockets. He leaned against the doorframe and smiled.

"Hi," he said casually.

I stood stunned. I wasn't expecting to see his face so early in the morning. He might be looking all perky and bright as he occupied my entryway, but I could tell from his bloodshot eyes and slight creases in his brow that he was nursing a serious hangover.

"Hello. And how are you feeling this morning?"

I didn't mean to sound so condescending, but I hadn't had my coffee yet.

"I was hoping you could tell me," he said with a boyish grin. "For some reason, I have a huge bump on my forehead and my shoulder kind of hurts. Why is that?"

Images of Joseph taking a face-plant in the hallway came to mind. I brought my hand up to my mouth to hide my amusement. "I can tell you exactly why that is. You passed out in the hallway, and it wasn't gracefully executed."

He hung his head and closed his eyes. His face furrowed a bit as he pondered his next words. "I don't remember much from last night, but I feel like I owe you an apology. Did you help me to my room after my swan dive?"

I crossed my arms, kind of proud of this moment. "I did."

He looked even more confused than before. "Did I ask you to?"

"I don't think so, but then again it was difficult to make out some of the things you said. I caught most of it though."

"I said things?" He swallowed. "To you?"

I nodded, knowing this was when he was about to make excuses for his drunken slips-of-the-tongue and that every bit of it was meant for Caroline. He stared at his feet with his hands now on his hips, his lips stretched to fine lines.

His next words floored me.

"I'm not going to apologize for what I said to you because I'm pretty sure whatever it was, I meant it. But I *am* going to say I'm sorry for interrupting your evening. I know you were entertaining your doctor...boxer friend, or whatever he was, and I hope I didn't ruin anything by dropping ass at your doorstep."

His choice of words cracked me up. "You didn't ruin anything." I rolled my eyes, kicking myself for concocting this ridiculous lie in the first place. "I didn't have a dinner date, and I don't know any doctors. Or boxers or bodybuilders, for that matter. I was home alone. So, quit your worrying. I was happy to help you."

I watched him cock his head to the side, his hair falling into his right eye. "You lied to me?"

I scratched my head, feeling the ground slipping from under me. "You believed me? I mean, come on...a bodybuilder slash doctor? Does that kind of person even exist? Surely, you were smart enough to see through that translucent veil of blatant deception."

I hated to do that. To take his accusation, though completely true, and turn it around on him. But this wasn't about me. This was about him invading my personal time and dumping his problems in my lap. I didn't want to be involved with this man or his convoluted issues of the heart.

"Right," he replied, seemingly at a loss for words. There might even been a little disappointment in his tone because I'd made him sound foolish, but I had to remind myself that it was all for the best.

"Well, I hope you feel better soon," I said, closing the door.

His hand stopped it. "I wasn't finished with you."

My mind downshifted into first gear. *Not finished with me? What did he mean by that?*

He took a gander past my shoulder into my apartment and breathed in. "Is that coffee?"

Lagging behind in the conversation, I tried to catch up with reality. "W-what did you ask? I'm sorry, I missed that."

He laughed. "I asked you if that was coffee I smell."

"Oh, yeah." I looked back toward my dreaded coffee maker. Pot was full, thank goodness. "Yeah, I'm making coffee. Would you like a cup?"

What are you doing, Jamie?

"Thanks, I could really use one."

Great. I just invited the man I was supposed to avoid into my apartment. An apartment cluttered with unpacked boxes of personal mementos. Where was my head?

Actually, this might work out perfectly. He'd see all the junk and chaos in my home, which was completely the opposite of his pristine living space, and run for the hills. I wouldn't have to break the news to him that I was uninterested, and he'd never feel the need to come over again.

Bingo!

"Please, come in," I offered with a pleasant smile.

As he stepped in, I could see he harbored a slight sense of fear, as if a booby trap were about to spring open on him. He scanned the room, taking in my mess. His thumbs were back in his front pockets, and he had a swagger in his stroll.

"Nice apartment," he complimented.

Liar.

"It looks like yours, but without all the disarray."

He turned to face me, his smile beaming bright. He seemed to enjoy the idea that I had been in his home, even if he didn't remember a single moment of my visit. I began to realize my plan for scaring him away wasn't working. He was tougher than I thought.

I ditched the original plan and headed for the coffee pot, having no idea how to drive him away. I was as skilled at being cold-hearted as I was at lying, so telling him he was too pretty to be my type was out of the question.

I shot him a quick look over my shoulder. He was eerily quiet, and I wondered if my untidiness was messing with his head. I raided the refrigerator for whipped cream and French vanilla creamer as he gazed up at the high ceilings, down the oversized windows, and around the open floor plan of the area.

His lips arched downward in thought. "They're similar apartments, yours and mine, but you've enhanced the appeal of some of my favorite things—mahogany wood, wrought iron, and leather. Are you an interior decorator?"

I wanted to laugh. I was a lot of things, but not a person who could beautify the indoors with color, texture, and design. My talents went as far as pressing a button on a machine and watching it brew the world's most beloved liquid.

"I appreciate the compliment, but I'm not an interior decorator."

"What *do* you do?" he asked, meeting me in the kitchen. He leaned across the island, his biceps bulging above the right angle of his arms. I tried to keep my focus on the technique of pouring two cups of coffee. When I scooped a huge dollop of whipped cream to top them off, he came off the counter.

"Whoa, whoa," he said, raising his hands. "What are you doing? You're ruining a perfectly good cup of coffee."

"I take it you like yours black?"

"I like mine the way Juan Valdez intended."

I recalled the vintage 1980s Columbian coffee commercial. I hadn't heard that name in forever, but I could still see the early riser slipping into his boots after the crow of a rooster and heading to the fields to pick the richest coffee in Columbia.

I handed him his mug and took a quick sip of mine, the cream settling on my upper lip. My tongue, licking it off, caught his attention. His eyes lingered on my mouth, but as soon as he realized I saw his drifting gaze, he looked away.

"So, what do you do again?" he asked, clearing his throat.

"I own a coffee shop on Fountain Square." I gave a wry smile. "I ruin hundreds of cups of coffee on a daily business."

"I Like You a Latte?" he asked, almost surprised. "That's your place?"

"Yes, it is. You've been there?"

"A few times," he admitted. "Guess I'll have to go more often now."

I bit my lip and felt the blood surface beneath my skin, my cheeks warming under his comment. As great as Joseph walking through the door of my café looked in my head, I wanted to change the subject. I didn't really like when it was on me. "So, what do *you* do for a living?"

He lifted the cup to his mouth, puckered his lips in the most alluring way as he blew the steam from the top and took his first sip. He seemed to enjoy the taste, savoring the comfort of the hot brew easing his hangover. "I do a lot for a living. Jack-of-all-trades kind of guy. Whatever comes up."

My spirits plummeted. I wasn't supposed to care about any of this because I wasn't getting involved. But like a sensible woman should, I always kept my options open and considered them with a frugal mind.

At least Joseph had a job.

Be that as it may, it sounded like he hopped from

opportunity to opportunity. Was it wrong of me to deduct a couple points from his tally because he was a drifter? Maybe. But I didn't like change, and Joseph clearly rolled with the punches on a frequent basis. That was not something I could mesh with easily.

Suddenly, I pictured him strumming out a tune on his guitar, a beautiful melody with heart and soul in every chord. I remembered Caroline and her critical remark about his songwriting. Perhaps he was a musician at heart and a blue-collar worker by trade, just until he could land his big break.

"So, how's the songwriting going?" I blurted without thinking. I wanted to kick myself.

His eyes leapt to mine, and he put on a serious mask. I buried my face in the mug so I didn't have to make eye contact with him, but I could feel the heat of his stare burning through my ceramic cup.

"I'm sorry, I shouldn't have pried."

"No, it's okay," he reassured kindly. "I just didn't know it was public knowledge."

"Well, with all due respect, anything said in an open hallway of an apartment complex is considered public."

His head tilted backward as he understood where I came from. "That's right...you were eavesdropping on my dispute with Caroline yesterday morning."

Sensations of heat prickled up my neck and enflamed my cheeks. "I wasn't eavesdropping,"

Joseph's smile returned. "Oh yeah? What do you call it then?"

I took a deep breath, hoping to redeem myself. "I call it being at the wrong place at the right time."

He reached out and clicked his mug with mine. "I'll drink to that."

I felt empowered by his simple toast and his cordial gesture. I felt I'd risen a few rungs on the caliber ladder, nearing his level of acceptance. We seemed to be genuinely enjoying each other's company, despite the awkwardness of how we first met. I was ready to relax a little in his presence.

"Do you want to sit down?" I motioned toward the dinner table. I slipped into my normal spot, and he found his across from me. Before I could get comfortable, he dropped a question into my lap.

"So, why did you lie to me?"

I wasn't prepared for this. "Excuse me?"

"You said you had dinner plans last night. A date. Why did you say that? What was the point?"

I stared into my cup for answers. Not one floated to the top. "I don't know. I guess I thought you were pretending to have a date too, so I did the same."

"But I *did* have a date. Well, plans," he reminded as he took another sip. "I was in a tie, remember."

"For all I knew, you could have been coming back from work, just as I was doing."

Joseph narrowed his eyes on me. "For future reference, I never wear a tie to work."

"Good to know. But just to reiterate, I didn't know it then. You were a stranger."

"I'm still a stranger." His flirty smile shot straight through my heart.

"Not really. Would a stranger know the color of your sheets, the size of your shoes, and a tiny tattoo on your right wrist with the initials L.M.S written in a script-like heart?"

Joseph's laughter echoed throughout the room. "Touché, Sutherland."

At the instant he spoke my surname, I realized I didn't know his. I was also curious about the initials he choose to permanently ink on his body, but figured that question would have to wait for a later date. "Since we've graduated from strangers to acquaintances, do I get the privilege of knowing your full name?"

He slouched back in his chair and stretched his legs out in front of him. "Joseph Alexander Scarbrough. Named after my grandfather."

"I like it," I said sincerely. "It's sounds regal and chivalrous."

Again he laughed. "I don't think anyone who knows me would knight me under those traits."

"What about Caroline?" I dared to mention the ex. I couldn't help it. I wanted to know how he felt about her. "A woman like her doesn't give her heart away to just anyone. Surely, she found a redeeming characteristic in your personality."

The way a man talks about his ex-girlfriend was a good indicator of what kind of person he was. If he belittled her and had nothing but bad things to say about her, then he was liable to be judgmental, insensitive, and rude. I was hoping Joseph was none of those things. I waited for his answer with baited breath.

"Caroline might have thought I hung the moon when we were younger, but I guess she's not that impressed these days."

I lifted my cup to my lips, pondering Joseph's bleak outlook. While he didn't exactly insult Caroline, he didn't offer a kind word about her either. Hmm…I was still on the fence. Teetering, but still on it.

Joseph stood up from the table. "May I?" he asked, thumbing toward the coffee pot.

"Sure," I said, staggering out of my thoughts. I glanced

into my cup. "I'll need some too."

He brought the pot with him and poured my cup first. *What a gentleman.* As he filled his, he returned to the previous subject. "I suppose I can't blame her though. I tried to be there for her. I really did. But I guess she needed more than I could give." Eventually, he sat back down at the table and stared out the ten-foot windows lining the south wall. "She's better off finding someone else."

"Why do you say that?" The look he gave me sent my heart aflutter.

"Because I'd only hold her back. I can't fall in love. I've tried. I thought it would be easy with Caroline, since we were childhood friends and I knew her so well. For years, I tried to let myself fall. But it's never happened. I don't think it ever will."

If I were a woman on the prowl, I would have taken Joseph's words as a dare and set my mind to proving him wrong. Whether he meant it that way or not, any woman with a pulse would have already started plotting her next move to make this guy fall in love. Fortunately for me, I was not one of those women, and I could easily disregard the temptation of setting my sights on this handsome test subject. I had better things to do with my life than woo a man incapable of love just for the sake of saying it could be done.

All betting aside though, I had to admit for a second I flirted with the idea of trying.

Chapter Six

My day took quite a turn. I'd gone from shy and reserved to comfortable and giggling in the span of a few hours. Joseph and I had finished one pot of coffee and were halfway into the next, digging through my unpacked boxes.

I knew this stuff was supposed to be my personal stash of childhood memories and trinkets, but when Joseph asked me about them, I had no choice but to come clean. As I was spooning more whipped cream into my coffee in the kitchen, he peered inside one of the boxes and inquired about its contents. I expected him to ridicule me for the odd assortment of saved items, but *au contraire*! He pulled out my collection of cassette tapes and marveled over them, as if I'd stockpiled objects from a sunken treasure.

"Oh, my gosh, you have Hootie & The Blowfish and Radiohead? I haven't heard these guys in forever." Joseph opened the case as if he had to see it to believe it. "I used to play their songs all the time in my garage when the band would get together to practice. My mom hated it."

He smiled as if he enjoyed ticking his mother off.

"You played in a band?" I wasn't questioning him out of disbelief. He owned a guitar and wrote songs, so the organized musician thing wasn't a far fetch. But I longed to know all there was to know about Joseph.

For purely conversational reasons, of course, I reminded myself.

"Yeah," he said reminiscently. "We called ourselves 'The Best the World Has Ever Seen.'"

We both laughed at the idiosyncratic stage name. I could just picture him standing at the microphone with his guitar strapped to his body, his fist high in the air as he announced the group's alias. I wondered if he sang the songs he wrote, or if he was just lead guitar.

"That's quite a mouthful,"

"Yes it was," he concurred. "But it's a name you'd never forget. Right?"

"I'll give you that."

I sat cross-legged on the floor wearing nothing but baggy sweats and a ponytail, drinking coffee, talking and laughing with a guy I had never expected to give me the time of day. It felt amazing to hang out with someone, particularly a male, without feeling the need to impress. Was I dreaming? No way. It couldn't be a dream. My heart sang, and my face hurt from smiling so much.

A few more hours passed by, and a few more boxes had been emptied. Somehow I had Joseph carrying boxes to the dumpster and a couple to his truck to donate to Goodwill. With his help, I'd been able to go through each one, decide the fate of its contents, pack the keepers away, and trash the rest. I'd rid my apartment of the clutter, and my to-do-list had been completely checked off.

Melissa would be so surprised. Not only for unpacking the rest of the boxes, but unpacking the rest of the boxer while hanging out with Joseph. I could just hear her now. *You mean you turned me down for a hunky, songwriting neighbor with beautiful biceps and great hair?* I could see her giving me another one of her disco bumps and adding *Don't sweat it, darlin'. I would have too.* A high-pitched squeal would likely follow, along with her begging for the dirty details.

"Oh, if only I had some to offer," I muttered under my breath, as I finished the last of the dishes.

"If only you had what to offer? And to whom?"

I gasped and turned around at the sound of Joseph's voice as he re-entered the apartment. I had no idea he had returned so quickly from the garbage run. I fished for a properly evasive reply. "Um…If only I had some donuts to offer. To you. You know, coffee and donuts…they go great together."

He approached the island and sat at one of the stools.

"Don't give me some lame defense, Jamie. I know what I heard. You were talking to yourself, and I don't think it had anything to do with donuts."

I sighed and unplugged the drain, drying my hands on the nearby towel. "I was just imagining what my friend, Melissa, would say on Monday morning when I tell her that I've officially unpacked everything. So, there."

"And…"

"And that the person who helped me was not her, but you."

"She was supposed to help you?"

"Not exactly," I amended. "She's offered to help me many times, but I've always declined."

"I see." He folded his hands on the counter. "So, what do you wish you had to offer her?"

I turned around, hiding my embarrassment. There was no way I could face this man while confessing the truth. "After Melissa learns I had a man in my apartment, she's the type of girl who'll want details. You know, the dirty details. More explicit the better."

I felt his presence behind me. I hadn't expected him to ditch his place at the counter and approach me so daringly. "You mean details like, how close I stood to you when I said goodbye? Or whether or not I kissed you before I left?"

I swallowed.

Hard.

I couldn't breathe. I couldn't think about anything but Joseph behind me. He turned me around and lifted my chin with the curve on his index finger. The simple contact he made with my face rooted me to the floor. His hand felt warm against my skin, and I could smell the faint aroma of last night's cologne swirling around me.

He tested me, this I knew, but my normal brain function took a hiatus. I was left with nothing but my own addlebrained thoughts and emotions, neither of which could save me from the intensity of this moment.

I saw a glint of amusement in his eyes. The corner of his mouth twitched into a smile. "How about you let me take you out tonight, and we'll see if we can muster up some of those details your friend might ask for."

"Like a date?" I asked stupidly.

He released me and crossed his arms, leaning against the refrigerator. Satisfaction beamed from every aspect of his face. From the twinkle in his eyes, to the depth of his laugh lines, he looked very proud of himself. "Yes, like a date. Will you let me take you out, you know, since we're no longer strangers."

A thousand thoughts ran through my mind. Indeed, we were no longer strangers, per se, but I couldn't forget that he had newly separated from his girlfriend. A little over twenty-four hours was not long enough for anyone to get over a break-up. At this stage in the game, I'd be nothing but the rebound girl.

"Okay," he stated, holding up his hands. "I can see I've put you on the spot and you're worried I'm moving too quickly. I mean, Caroline just left me yesterday morning and I'm already asking you out on a date. I get that. But here's the thing. I'm not asking you out so I can pursue you."

You're not? The question echoed in my head. *Then what are you doing?*

"I'm asking a woman I really enjoy being around to spend some time with me."

I blinked in rapid succession. I had no idea if I was supposed to be happy or disappointed about his platonic objective.

"I like you, Jamie," he concluded. "I like talking with you and hanging out. I've never had someone I could be this comfortable around. It's nice. And I think you feel the same."

Again, I was dumbfounded. I could hardly catch up. I was still stuck at *I like you, Jamie.*

He checked his watch. "It's only four o'clock. You've got time to think about it, and I've got time to make some plans. If you decide you'd like to take me up on my offer, knock on my door. If not, then so be it. No hard feelings."

He winked at me and casually walked out.

Chapter Seven

I threw out my arms and braced myself between the island and the sink counter. The earth-shattering invitation Joseph had challenged me with softened the bones of my legs into spaghetti noodles. I said 'challenged' because everything about his offer was just that. It was a challenge to think clearly. It was a challenge to know whether he had ulterior motives behind the date. It was a challenge to forget the way his touch felt upon my skin and the things my body felt because of it. And let's not forget, it was also a challenge to turn him down.

While I reminded myself that accepting his offer was a huge mistake, I wanted nothing more than to rip open my door, chase after him, and scream *yes* at the top of my lungs. It was not every day a woman like me would get a chance to be with a man like Joseph. He was strikingly handsome, confident, and mysterious. He had the power to look through me when he gazed into my eyes, but I'd be darned if I could read his. He held himself with as much poise as a wealthy aristocrat, but without conceit and preeminence. And he listened to me when I spoke as if he hung on my every word.

No man had ever done that.

I took a deep breath and exhaled slowly, counting the seconds until I completely expelled all the air in my lungs. I tried to force myself to relax, to convince my scarred heart that it had nothing to worry about. Oh, how I tried, but it had been broken too many times not to fret about old wounds and the pain of reopening them.

I gathered some leftover strength and walked over to the window. The sun had begun to set over the Covington skyline. Daylight savings time had ended a few weeks ago, and the last bit of sunlight struggled to illuminate the riverfront.

Dusk was the time when the city came alive. The B&B riverboats cruised up and down the Ohio, and Newport on the Levee lit up with local bands playing on the banks and people dancing on the walkways beneath the flickering Christmas lights tightly woven around the bare trees. Fountain Square would be crawling with holiday shoppers, kissing couples, and festive friends painting the town red.

I imagined being out amongst the crowds, Joseph at my side. I could see his smile and hear his laughter over the jazz band playing on the corner. I could feel the warmth of his hand around mine as he led me down the busy sidewalks toward the special place he planned to take me. I could see myself enjoying his company and having the best night of my life.

If only I said 'yes.'

What stopped me? The idea of Joseph rebounding for starters. I understood he felt unwanted and I made him feel desirable again, but that didn't make it right for him to use me to get over Caroline.

Another big reason I hesitated was because I didn't want to get hurt. I'd been in the committed relationship scene before. This wasn't my first rodeo. But with each go-round, I'd been thrown from the saddle, eaten dirt, my heart broken, my pride bruised. I had dusted myself off so many times that getting back on that temperamental horse had no appeal to me anymore. I feared one more wild ride would darn near kill me.

The last and biggest obstacle I had for steering clear of Joseph was that my life didn't have room to accommodate him. I had my routines, my rituals, the things I did each day that kept me focused and sane. Having someone like Joseph, who probably flew by the seat of his pants all the time, would throw a serious monkey wrench in my predictable existence.

I didn't adapt well to change. When things in my life were modified or altered at a moment's notice, I felt like my world was spinning out of control. I had to have my hands on the wheel at all times, at ten and two. No surprises, no compromises. It was the way I liked it.

I looked toward the door of my apartment. Beyond the wood of that two-inch barrier laid an opportunity to be someone else. To do something different. To have something new.

My heart skipped a beat. I had no way of knowing whether its rampant rhythm was coerced by the anxiety of the unknown or the excitement of the thrill. The comfort of predictability usually kept my pulse at an even pace, but right now it pounded so wildly against my ribs, I thought it might burst from my chest.

I stood up, throwing my hands above my head in surrender. "All right! I'll do it!"

I ran for the door, delighted by my impulsive decision. I gripped the handle and jerked it open. The sound of a woman's voice stopped me in my tracks.

I peeked into the hallway and saw Caroline stomping toward the elevator, Joseph on her heels.

"Caroline, wait."

I closed the door enough that no one would notice it ajar, but left it open enough so I could still hear. I knew it was wrong to eavesdrop on their private conversation—again—but I had to. I was not about to run to Joseph, ready to accept his offer with foolhardy exuberance, if he intended to jump back into a relationship with her.

My heart skidded to a halt, preparing for the usual disappointment I came to expect with men. I held my breath, waiting to hear what Joseph had to say.

"Caroline, listen to me." His voice sounded desperate, and the elevator door took the brunt of his command as I heard him forcibly slide it back open. I envisioned him holding it with a strong arm. "We've known each other since we were kids. Doesn't that count for something?"

My spirits plummeted. He wanted her back. I should have known.

Close the door and save yourself from hearing the rest.

I ignored the voice in my head. I had to be sure how he felt about her. He, at least, owed me that much.

"I can't be friends with you, Joseph," Caroline snapped. "It would be too hard for me to see you with someone else."

"There *is* no one else."

"There will be," she laughed sardonically. "There always is. You never stay unattached for long."

"Don't do this," he begged.

"Joseph, you did this."

"How? What did I do that made you feel you have to walk away from what we've always had?"

"That's just it. We have nothing because you refused to give all of yourself. Ever since your sister died, you've built these walls around your heart, and no one is strong enough to tear them down. Not even me, the girl you've known all your life."

I pressed further against the door, not wanting to miss his next words. The identity of those tattooed initials on his wrist suddenly became apparent.

"So, our life-long friendship means nothing to you?"

I couldn't see either of them or how close they were to each other, but I imagined Joseph's spellbinding eyes boring into her soul. Caroline was sure to give in now.

"It means the world to me, but I want more. I *deserve* more. Damn, Joseph, I've spent all of my childhood chasing you, crushing on you. You say you want to love me, but you won't let yourself. You won't give me any more than what everyone else gets."

"It's difficult for me, you know that. But just because I can't love you like you want me to, doesn't mean we have to throw everything away We've been the best of friends since we were kids."

"If I can't have your heart, then I refuse to waste any more of my life with you."

"So, this is it?" he asked, his voice cracking. "You're going to throw away our friendship over…" He never got to finish. Caroline said her goodbye over his plea, and I heard the elevator close with a ding.

I listened intently. I wondered if he was the type of guy to chase after her and beg for another chance. I wondered if he wanted to.

A loud bang startled me as if he'd struck his fist against the wall, and the sound of solid footsteps approached. I quietly pushed the door the rest of the way closed, holding the handle at full-twist so it wouldn't generate a click on the hinges.

In a few seconds, a slamming door echoed down the hall. I breathed a heavy respire, my heart in my throat.

What do I do now?

Chapter Eight

I stood at my door for what seemed like an eternity. Should I act like I didn't hear anything that had transpired down the hall and knock on Joseph's door anyway? Maybe he'd be too upset to go out, and he'd have to figure out how to renege on his offer without feeling like a jerk. Or maybe I should knock on his door, like a good friend would, and just be there for him.

There was no doubt he needed someone right now. Caroline had ripped his heart from his chest and left him to bleed. If anyone knew what he was going through, it was me. I had been left for dead countless times with no one to sop up the blood or stitch the gaping wounds.

I may have only known Joseph for a day, but I was the closest thing he had to a loyal friend. I would not let him suffer alone.

I swung open the door and froze. Joseph stood there, his fist suspended in the air as if he were about to knock. Our eyes met, and for once the mystery vanished. I read the emotions behind his eyes, as if they were flashing neon lights.

Sadness, the kind that was deep-seated and destructive, pervaded every inch of his persona. He stood with his back hunched, his chin lowered, and his confidence in shambles. The luster in his sapphire eyes had dulled to a gloomy shade of grey. He forced a smile, though I saw through his façade, for I'd done the same many times.

"Hey," he said, shuffling his feet. "We seem to be doing this a lot lately."

I gave my warmest smile, hoping it would dissolve some of the awkwardness between us. "Yeah, we do."

I thought he'd make up some excuse as to why he suddenly had to cancel the date. I'd be okay with that, for I'd never want a pity date anyway. What I *did* want was to take his pain away. To reach out, wrap my arms around his neck, and squeeze for all I was worth. The notion of never letting go sounded even better. I imagined Joseph had the best hugs in the world. Strong and secure.

I could give him that too. I wanted to give him that, but I stood motionless. My nerve had been shot full of holes. The way he looked at me caused my backbone to lose its resolve. The sadness I initially saw in his eyes faded away. His chin had lifted slightly and so had the corners of his lips.

He scoffed aloud and shook his head.

"What?" I asked, priming myself for the let down.

"I was going to tell you something," he said earnestly, "but I completely forgot what it was. You do that to me, you know?"

"Do what?" My curiosity spun into overdrive.

"Make me lose my head."

I apologized, though I wasn't sure why.

"Don't be sorry," he coaxed. "I don't mind. Seeing you…" He fished for the right words. "…helps."

"But you've only been gone a few moments." I decided not to let on I'd overheard their conversation in the hall. For the sake of his injured pride, I thought it best.

"I know I just left, but…"

He furrowed his brow, as if sorting through his emotions. Men didn't typically know how to come to terms with their innermost feelings. I figured Joseph was no different. So, I helped him along.

"Did you need something?"

"What?"

I had to smile at the pure, unadulterated ditziness he suddenly had. "You came back after offering to take me out. I was supposed to knock on *your* door, if I decided to take you up on your invitation. Did you forget something?"

I allowed him enough time to catch up. Apparently, his blond moment was short lived. "No, I didn't leave anything behind. But…" he pointed at me and smiled. "You were headed out this door right before I knocked. Should I assume you were coming to knock on my door?"

He had me. I fidgeted with my hands, brushing a few strands of hair out of my eyes. "Maybe."

He hiked his arm above his head and leaned his forearm on the doorframe, crossing his ankles casually. Little by little, the Joseph I'd spent the entire day with came back. Had I brought about this change in him? Was simply being around me enough to place his heart on the mend?

I certainly gave myself a lot of credit. It made more sense to think Joseph was no stranger to such tragedies. Take losing his sister for instance. Joseph seemed like the kind of man who'd shake off his afflictions and carry on.

I eyed him carefully, uncertain of the right words. "Let's say, hypothetically, I was coming to knock on your door. And you were on the other side of that door, where you were supposed to be."

"Go on."

"Would you be happy in hearing a rap upon your door? Or would you be burdened by it? Tell me the truth."

"You want the honest-to-God's truth, Jamie?"

My heart gave out for a second. I wondered whether I could physically handle the truth, should the truth be detrimental to my self-esteem. Depending on what he said, he might find me collapsed at his feet in a fetal position, protecting myself from further psychological damage. Just thinking about it had me breaking out into a cold sweat. I suddenly felt dizzy. My hands began to shake.

"Yes," I said wearily. "I want the honest-to-God's truth."

He stepped toward me and reached for my hands. The zing of his touch jolted up my arms and ricocheted throughout my body. The energy he supplied to every axon in my central nervous system went into complete overload.

"If you knocked on my door, I'd be so happy, I might even kiss you."

That was the last thing I remembered before everything went black.

Chapter Nine

My eyes fluttered open, and Joseph's beautiful face stared at me. He looked concerned, if my frazzled brain was registering correctly, and I wondered what had happened.

I could feel something soft beneath me, as if I were lying down. But with the shock of opening my eyes to the sexiest man in the world only inches from me, I had no idea where I was. I tore my eyes from his gaze and checked my surroundings. The familiarity of my living room comforted me to some extent, but knowing Joseph had probably carried me in his arms and laid me on my couch unsettled me. I had no recollection of it, and I could kick myself. It wasn't every day that a woman found herself in the arms of a desirable man.

"Are you all right?" he asked, brushing back a strand of my hair.

I blinked away the fuzziness of my thoughts and shook my head. "What happened? Did I just pass out?"

"Yeah, you did," he replied softly. "I caught you before you hit the floor, but I admit I wasn't prepared for it." He tilted his head to the side, observing me closely. "I'm going to go out on a limb here and assume you have low blood sugar?"

I clenched my tingling hands into tight balls, my mind still a bit sluggish. I hated this feeling when it came on. "How did you know?"

"My friend Greg has the same problem. He usually warns me before he drops to the floor though."

I closed my eyes, feeling exhausted. After a bout of my sugar crashing, I was practically useless. I tried to muster some energy, but none was available to me.

"Jamie," I heard him call to me.

"Mm-hmm…"

"Open your eyes and look at me."

I obeyed him, even though all I wanted to do was sleep.

"You need to eat something."

"I'm not hungry."

"Tough," he said, taking me by the arms and lifting me to a sitting position. He pulled me closer to him on the couch and steadied me. "I hope you don't mind, but I took the liberty of rummaging through your kitchen for food. Here." He tore open the wrapper of a chocolate covered granola bar and shoved it in my hand. "While looking for this, I also found about five take-out menus from Thai joints. I assume that means you like Thai, so I ordered us some. It should be here soon. In the meantime, drink some orange juice. Again, I'm taking a stab here, but is that what I chased all those oranges for?"

"Yeah." A sudden smile pierced my lips as I remembered Joseph's hot pursuit down the hall. "Oranges help to maintain sugar levels once they're back up."

Joseph laughed. "Oh, now you decide to be all smart and doctor-like. Where was this woman who should've remembered this while drinking tons of coffee with nothing to eat all day?"

That woman was totally preoccupied, I thought inwardly, recalling the immense fun I had in his company. I made the decision not to give him an answer and save face. I drank the entire glass of the freshly-squeezed juice and glanced at him over the rim. I noticed he was still watching me closely.

"I'm fine," I insisted. "You don't have to keep doing that."

"Doing what?"

"Monitoring me like I'm some helpless child you need to keep an eye on."

"Maybe I like keeping an eye on you."

I rolled my eyes. His statement would have sounded so much better to my ears had I not made a spectacle of myself beforehand.

The buzzer erupted through the apartment, splitting my head in two.

"That was fast," Joseph said, standing. He gave me a quick once-over. "Will you be all right while I'm gone?"

I crowded my brows in confusion.

"Thai's here," he said pointing toward the door. "I gotta go let the guy in the building and pay him. You all right?"

My memory came back to me. Right. Joseph ordered take-out. I nodded my head and took another bite of the granola bar.

He backed out of the living room and pointed at me, his boyish grin tickling my insides. "Don't go anywhere."

I feigned a smile on the outside, but inside I was darn near humiliated. Why did this man have to see me in my most vulnerable state, and why in the world was he sticking around?

During his absence, those questions continued to roll through my mind, especially after knowing his childhood sweetheart decided to give up on their friendship. I didn't know that much about Joseph, but I assumed he wasn't as strong as he was acting. If someone had done that to me, I would have been devastated. From the look on his face when I had opened the door and found him about to knock, he looked quite upset by the turn of events.

I then recalled what he'd said to me thereafter. *I was going to tell you something, but I completely forgot what it was. You do that to me, you know? Make me lose my head.*

I couldn't help but feel special. I'd made this guy lose his train of thought. He didn't appear to be a man who'd let anyone get into his head on such a profound level, no matter who they were. He had too much self-assurance to be that weak.

Yet, he admitted to being wounded. *Seeing you…helps.*

Again, I felt exceptionally special to have alleviated whatever strife he was going through, even if I had no clue what he really meant by the statement. Realizing the mammoth smile on my face, I quickly took another bite of the granola bar. The last thing I wanted to do was have him catch me in the act of enjoying his downfall.

Thank goodness I took control of my emotions when I did, for he walked in unannounced, a large white sack in one hand, keys in the other, and a small bag hanging from his teeth. He smiled the minute he saw me and kicked the door shut.

"Dinner is served," he muttered, still clenching the bag between his lips.

He sat beside me, and I reached for it. "What's this?"

"Extra fortune cookies," he winked. "I figured there's nothing wrong with stocking up on a little more luck."

"More luck?"

"Yeah," he said, tearing into the take-out bag. "I lost one friend and gained another all in the same day. How many times does that happen to a person?"

I knew the question was purely rhetorical, but I silently agreed with him. If anyone was lucky this weekend, it was me. When it came to good fortune, most times it would pass me right by. Someone must have slipped Mr. Sandman a missive. Either that or he tripped and spilled his magic dust all over me by accident.

"Don't worry," he interrupted my thoughts. "I'll share with you."

"You think I need some added luck in my life?"

"I know you do," he concluded. "You're contending with me in your life, all of a sudden, and I doubt it was something you planned. If that isn't bad luck, I don't know what is."

I opened the Styrofoam container and regarded Joseph's choice of words. "I wouldn't call it 'contending.'"

I watched as Joseph helped himself to a set of chopsticks and deftly lifted his first bite to his mouth. He proved to be skilled with the utensils and a sense of wonder overtook me. I, on the other hand, had never gotten the hang of them despite my many futile attempts.

"So, what would you call it?" he asked.

I speculated whether to try the chopsticks in front of him or just concede to using the fork provided for me by the sympathetic owners of the Thai restaurant. I chickened out. I ripped open the sheer plastic covering on the fork and dove in. "I call it opening a door for a friend in need."

Joseph nodded, but he seemed lost in thought, toying with his rice and vegetables.

"You don't believe me?" I asked.

His eyes landed on mine in a way that froze every muscle in my body.

"No, I believe you, Jamie. But I can't help but think if you hadn't known about Caroline walking out on me yesterday morning, you wouldn't have opened that door at all. You wouldn't have picked me up off the hallway floor and put me into my bed after my drunken binge. And I doubt you would have invited me in for coffee the next morning."

"You think I did all that out of pity?"

"Honestly, I don't know why you did it."

I took a deep breath and prepared my response in my head. Truth be told, I couldn't say I had a logical explanation for why I helped him in so many ways. Sure, assisting a beautiful man like Joseph had its perks, especially for a single woman looking to score a new man, but that was not me. I didn't lend a hand to him because I aimed to cut forward in line of all the other women in his life. Just thinking that had me cringing.

"Well?" he encouraged.

I straightened my back and looked him square in the eye. "I did it because that is how I'm made. I don't turn my back on those in need." I stuck my fork deep into the pile of spicy goodness, on the verge of saying more. I bit my lip, hesitating to open the dam of my convoluted mind. I had so much in my head he didn't need to hear, but I decided to at least unplug a small portion of it. "I don't know if you've figured it out yet, but I'm not like Caroline."

As soon as I said it, I regretted the words. I couldn't look at him anymore and, frankly I wondered where in the world that daring side of me came from. I certainly hoped I hadn't insulted him. Caroline was someone he cared for, and, by attacking her dignity, I might have overstepped my bounds. Then again, I wasn't the insensitive wench who had attacked his heart with no concern for his feelings.

While two wrongs shouldn't make a right, I wanted him to realize that not all women were heartless and self-absorbed.

"No, you're nothing like Caroline," he admitted. "In fact, you're nothing like any of the women I've known."

I was not aware of the exact number of females he had encountered, but with Joseph's striking good looks and charming personality, I assumed they could at least fill a small stadium. "Coming from you, I'll take that as a compliment."

"Contrary to what you might think, I know enough about women being the only male amongst three sisters. Probably more than a man *should* know."

"Somehow, I don't think that was your only means of knowing the female mind."

He looked at me askance, a half-cocked grin lighting up his face. "Should I take that as a compliment as well?"

"You should. You're a very thoughtful, charismatic, handsome man. I can't imagine you having any trouble meeting women or keeping their interest, with or without your sisters' help."

His hearty laughter filled the room, which made me want to laugh with him, though I didn't find much humor in my flattering remark. I meant it. Joseph was every girl's dream, including mine had I been searching for a perfect mate.

"You need to eat more, Jamie," he said, gently elbowing my arm. "That sugar of yours is still too low, and you're talking out of your head again."

I giggled and picked up the small bag of fortune cookies. "Let's see what Confucius has to say about it." I dug into the bag and pulled out the first one. "You know how to read these, don't you?"

"There's a wrong way to read a fortune cookie?"

"Not a wrong way," I corrected. "Just a better way. It adds more spunk to the average philosophical crap they write on these things."

"Oh, yeah?" His face lit up as he swiveled his body in my direction. "How do we do that?"

I enjoyed how he assumed this would be a partnership in order to enhance the general, ambiguous predictions of a crunchy vanilla treat. I broke my cookie open and pulled out the slip of paper. "It's really quite simple. You just add 'in bed' at the end of the fortune."

"In bed," he repeated skeptically.

"Here, just listen to mine." I read it silently to see if it worked. Some fortunes didn't make sense with the addition, but most times it added a whole new take on the prophecy. Mine worked perfectly.

He who controls others may be powerful, but he who has mastered himself is mightier still...in bed.

Joseph almost choked on his food. His reaction was

priceless as he beat his chest, trying to clear his airway so he could continue laughing.

"See, I told you it made them better."

"You weren't lying," he concurred. Excitedly, he reached for his fortune cookie and cracked it open. I watched him glance over it, reading it ahead of time with the additional word choice. His brow lifted and a devilish grin took shape. I sat transfixed in his gaze. "Oh, this is a good one. I think it might even be better than yours."

"Let's hear it."

He cleared his throat as if he were about to give a presidential address.

Any activity becomes creative when the doer cares about doing it right, or better...in bed.

Had I not been battling hypoglycemia, my reaction would have been a bit more spirited. He was definitely correct...his was better than mine, and I think he worried that I would've been embarrassed with his insinuative fortune. Maybe in time he'd realize I was not a prude, like I envisioned his Caroline to be.

"Guess you'll never look at a fortune cookie the same

again, will you?" I resumed eating while he continued to smirk at the tiny paper.

"You got that right." He tucked the fortune in the front pocket of his jeans and watched me as I chewed. "Is it good? Did I order the right meal?"

Remembering my manners, I didn't want to talk with my mouth full. I simply nodded and hid my massive chews behind my hand. Before I could fork another hearty portion, he handed me the other set of chopsticks.

"Try eating with these. It tastes so much better."

I took a few seconds to finish chewing and swallowed. "I've tried a thousand times and can't figure them out."

"That's because you never had *me* show you. Here." He took hold of my hand in his, and placed my fingers properly on the sticks while giving me tips on how one stick stays stationery in my grasp. I tried to listen to his expert advice, but all I focused on was the feel of his warm hands on mine. His touch felt exquisite against my skin, and I couldn't keep myself from enjoying its effect on the rest of my body.

"You're trembling," he noticed. "You cold?"

"No," I dismissed too quickly, wishing I would have conceded with his observation.

"What's wrong?" he badgered sweetly, his eyes gazing into mine.

I had to look away. Normally, I could stare into Joseph's eyes forever, but this time he had my insides in complete turmoil. "It's my sugar, I think," I fibbed.

He seemed to believe me and gave me back the fork. "I'll let it slide this once because you need to eat. But the next time we have Thai, you're using chopsticks. Got it?"

Next time? There's going to be a next time?

My heart did a summersault triggered by the exuberant fluttering of butterflies in my stomach. I passed over his offer as though it were a normal, everyday proposal and included one of my own. "Fine. I'll use chopsticks from now on, if you promise to let me ruin your coffee the next time you're in my shop."

He extended his right hand immediately without hesitation. "Deal."

I accepted his hand, and we shook on it, his grip strong and compelling. Somehow, I felt as if we were shaking hands on a different pact all together. In securing two 'next times,' he seemed to welcome whatever the future might hold for us.

Chapter Ten

Within an hour, my sugar rose to its appropriate level, but my energy took a nosedive. By the time Joseph and I finished our meal, I had sunk to a state of exhaustion. I could no longer keep my eyes open, and I slouched into the cushion of the couch. Playing host was no longer in the cards.

"All right," Joseph stated soundly. "I'm outta here. It's obvious I'm boring you."

My head felt like a two-ton boulder, but I managed to open my eyes. "You're not boring me. I'm just sleepy."

I felt his hand on my knee, and my breath caught. "Don't think you're getting out of going out with me so easily. Clearly tonight is not the night, but I'm holding you to it, you hear me?"

"I hear you," I said, smiling from ear to ear.

"Tomorrow is Sunday, and I have plans, so I can't do it then. How about next weekend? You free?"

I had absolutely no idea what I was doing next weekend, but I was darn sure I could move things around if

I had plans. No way was I going to let this opportunity slip through my fingers. And not because I wanted to suddenly pursue him. Undoubtedly, we were two different people who wanted different things in life. I enjoyed his friendship, the conversations, and the company—nothing more.

"Next weekend sounds great. Should I knock?" I jested.

"No, we're passed that now. I'll pick you up at seven on Friday."

I repeated the time and date in my head. Between Joseph's hand still on my knee and the fogginess of fatigue, I made a serious mental note not to forget. "Got it."

I felt him stir on the couch and lifted my eyelids just enough to catch Joseph reaching for the blanket on the nearby chair. He spread the afghan over me and winked. "Sleep tight, Sutherland."

The synapses in my brain were no longer firing at optimum speed, but I could tell by the tone of his voice that he didn't really want to leave. Knowing what I'd heard between him and Caroline this evening, I worried he would go off and do something stupid again, like drink himself to death.

"Are you okay?" I asked as he approached the door.

He glanced over his shoulder for a brief moment then turned around to face me. "Yeah," he said with a pleasant smile on his face. "I'm good."

He stood there gazing at me, his thumbs finding a home in his front pockets. If I could have taken a picture of Joseph, it would have been right now, second only to the moment when he had donned the towel. I loved the casual poise of his character, the squared confidence in his shoulders contradicting the laxity of his grin.

"This very well could have been the second worse day of my life," he explained, looking down at his feet for a second. He took a deep breath, as if fighting off an emotion he likely wanted to keep buried, before he raised his head with conviction. "But you, Jamie, turned this day around. Thanks for…" He searched for the right words. "For everything. For being you."

My eyes remained open. There was no way I could close them now. I couldn't say I understood what just happened, but something definitely changed between us. Not being very skilled in the ways of men and women, I couldn't discern between casual friendliness and potentially connecting on a whole new level. I just knew I felt a foreign emotion taking root in my heart, and I think he did too.

He glanced down at the bag of fortune cookies and impulsively snagged one before backing up toward the door. He cracked it open, popped half the tasty cookie in his mouth and read the inscription to himself, his devilish smile reaching all the way to his eyes.

Curiosity got the better of me. "What's it say?"

He shook his head. "It's my fortune, not yours."

"That's not fair."

"Some other time, maybe," he said, tucking the strip of paper into his jeans pocket. "You need to sleep."

I hadn't the energy to argue with him. I felt my eyes begin to close.

"See you Friday, Jamie," was all I heard as he left the image of his glorious smile branded on my brain upon his departure. After the door closed, I fell into a deep sleep with the image of Joseph Alexander Scarbrough holding me in his arms.

* * * *

The next morning was like any other, except that my first thoughts were of Joseph and not coffee. I sat up and stretched the stiffness in my neck and back, cursing myself for sleeping on the couch instead of in my own comfortable bed. Lesson learned. Never crash on the couch when a two-thousand-dollar, pillow-top mattress is but a few feet away.

Walking to the kitchen, I prepared to make my morning java. Joseph's lovely male voice unreeled itself in my head as I relived yesterday's key moments. The first that came to mind was his innocent grin the moment I opened the door before he could knock. His hair was adorably disheveled and his eyes bloodshot. It made me want to reach out and tame his silky, brown waves, to brush that pesky unruly lock away from his right eye.

The second memory was waking up from my hypoglycemic episode with his face inches from mine. Still groggy from my restless sleep, my overactive imagination led me past the boundaries of reality and into the realm of fantasy. Before I knew it, in my mind I had pressed my lips to Joseph's and kissed him.

The moment our lips met, I gasped and rewound myself to the present. I touched my mouth. The feel of Joseph's, or rather what I imagined his lips to feel like, lingered on mine. I could almost smell him.

Until the phone rang.

Irritated, I picked up my cell and answered. "Hello." I tried not to sound miffed, but darn it, it was difficult to break away from my morning reflections, even if they were fictitious.

Donna, my weekend college employee from the shop, divulged the madness she had endured upon opening, blathering on about how the espresso machine was not working properly. Rubbing my temples, I assured her that I would be right there to look at it. She seemed relieved to know I was coming but continued to apologize for calling on the weekend.

After a few moments of reassuring her, I hung up and threw on some clothes. Nothing special—just sweats and a T-shirt. Within ten minutes, I had brushed my teeth, combed my hair, slipped my arms inside my coat, and walked out the door.

As soon as I stepped into the corridor, something hard and unforgiving rammed into my leg. The awful sound of metal crashing resounded around me. I'd collided into someone passing by. I nearly buckled from the blow, but a pair of strong arms caught me before I went down.

"Oh, my gosh. Are you all right?"

I looked up and there stood Joseph, cradling me in his embrace. He looked just as handsome as he always did, but this time he wore jeans, work boots, and a tan Carhartt jacket. He smelled of soap and aftershave, yet the stubble on his face proved it was just for the aroma.

"I'm so sorry," he apologized, standing me on my own two feet. "We've got to stop meeting like this."

I glanced at the floor in the hallway. His faded-red, metal toolbox lay toppled on its side and I finally realized what had hit me. Until I looked away from Joseph, I hardly felt the pain in my thigh. Now it throbbed and burned. I reached down and gave it a good rub.

Joseph dropped to his knees and shimmied the elastic hem of my sweat pants halfway up my leg to inspect the damage. His fingers brushed the sensitive skin behind my knee, and my stance faltered a second time. I backed away from him. "I'm fine, Joseph. Really."

"You've got a welt the size of Antarctica on your thigh and a bruise already forming."

"It's okay," I assured him. "I bruise easily."

He stood and ran his fingers through his hair. "I'm serious, Jamie. I think I need to take you to the hospital. Those Champion toolboxes are made to take a beating."

I hopped on my injured leg, demonstrating that he'd not broken any bones and a trip to the hospital was unnecessary. "I'm not going to the ER for a bruise, Joseph. Now quit worrying." Ignoring the ache setting in, I bent to pick up his toolbox. It was a lot heavier than I expected and the lift became more of a heave. "Where are you headed?"

Joseph immediately seized it from my possession, his concern still visibly present in his eyes. "To my sister's farm. She's got a leaky barn roof."

This was the first I'd heard of his family. I couldn't help but be intrigued. "Your sister lives on a farm?"

"My whole family does. They're in the horse boarding business. It's pretty lucrative in Lexington."

"Is that where her farm is?"

He smiled, almost as if I were the first person to have taken an interest in his family's life. "Yeah, you want to come with me? I could use an extra hand."

My brain instantly crumbled to pieces in my head. I stumbled on my words and my tongue felt like it had been sailor-knotted. I couldn't believe he invited me to go to his family's residence. Most men are reluctant to take a new woman into their comfort zone, but Joseph didn't appear to care.

"I-I wish I could," I stammered. "But I've got to go into work. Espresso machine is pitchin' a fit today."

"I could take a look at it," he offered. "Got everything I'd need for the job right here."

For some reason, Joseph looked so much larger today. It might have been the bulky coat he wore or the extra inch of tread lining the bottom of his boots, but I swear he towered over me in this hallway. I stepped back to keep my head from tilting at such a steep angle.

"Oh, that's all right. You've got your hands full already. Besides, it might be a complicated job. I'll just call the repairman."

"On a Sunday? Seriously, it's no trouble."

I tried to dissuade him with another pitiful excuse, but he wouldn't budge.

He placed his hand on the small of my back and ushered me to the elevator. "Look, it's simple. We'll drive down to the shop and take a look at the machine. If it's an easy fix, we can be out the door and at my sister's in less than two hours. If it's a job above my qualifications, then you can call a repairman and decide what you want to do with your day from there. At least, let me give you a ride to work."

I broke. It was so easy to give in when it came to Joseph. Honestly, he could have threatened that spending the day with him would result in head-to-toe splinters, and I'd still want to come along.

Chapter Eleven

I'm not certain why I felt embarrassed about walking into my own coffee shop with Joseph at my heels. If anything, I should have felt proud to have this caliber of man in my company. Any woman would.

Not me.

All I felt was everyone's eyes on me, judging me, callously calculating how a guy like him could be with a girl like me and betting on how short the relationship would last. Little did they know there was no relationship to wager against.

I ignored the looks from all the female clientele sitting at the café tables and ushered Joseph behind the counter, removing my coat and gloves. Donna's eyes lit up when she saw me, but didn't remain on me for long. Her gaze automatically lifted above my shoulder to Joseph. She didn't say a word, but I could tell she longed for an introduction.

"Donna, this is Joseph," I said out of politeness. "He's my neighbor and pretty good with his hands."

She tore her eyes from his and gawked at me.

"I mean, he's good at fixing things," I corrected immediately. I pinched my nose, trying to gain some sort of composure in front of my hired help. "He's offered to look at the espresso machine."

Donna held out her hand and smiled warmly. "Wonderful," she said, shaking Joseph's hand. "I hope it doesn't give you as much trouble as it's given me this morning."

Joseph didn't look intimidated. If anything, he looked more determined than ever to repair the temperamental appliance. I directed him to the back counter and acted the informant, pointing out the fussy apparatus in question.

Joseph removed his jacket and handed it to me. My eyes fell over his broad shoulders and the muscles of his arms bulging beneath his tight cotton shirt. He didn't notice me staring, thank goodness, and for a short moment I got to take in his little Wrangler behind as he looked over the machine. That is until I noticed Donna waving her hand in front of her face as if too cool herself.

"Oh. My. Gosh," she mouthed.

I agreed with her silent, yet exaggeratedly expressive outburst. We exchanged a collective biting of our bottom lips and pretended to carry on with other duties, all the while sneaking glances at his beautiful body. I was taught better than to treat a man like a piece of meat, but I couldn't help it. Men like Joseph didn't come along every day, nor did they often award us with opportune moments of unabashed ogling. I told myself that one day he would move on to other more important escapades and our platonic relationship would fall by the wayside. I was only gorging my undue fill of him while I had the chance.

Donna slithered up next to me at the cash register. "Where did you find *this* guy?" she whispered as she wiped the already clean counter.

I glimpsed over my shoulder in Joseph's direction, hoping he hadn't heard her nosy inquiry. He had already unscrewed the back portion of the machine and was checking the hoses and the other intricate parts of the pesky contraption's innards. "Like I told you before, he's my neighbor."

"I wanna live where you live," she replied enthusiastically. "Course, I'd be purposefully running out of condiments just so I could knock on his door every night. Is he dating anyone?"

I looked at her curiously. Donna never had much to say to me in the past given the age gap between us. She was in her third year of college and I was in my early thirties, not to mention that I was her employer. But today, I didn't think I could shut her up if I duct taped her mouth closed.

I noticed the peculiar twinkle in her eye as she waited to hear about Joseph's availability. I was not a jealous person by nature, but something inside me hatched and chipped away my fragile exterior, daring to emerge. An inherent fem fatale-like possessiveness urged me to claim Joseph for myself. I cleared my throat and suppressed my sinister compulsions. I would not be guided down a gluttonous path. Though it pained me to remember his timely fall out with Caroline, I spoke the truth. "No, he's not dating anyone."

Donna sucked in a sharp breath and moved closer. "You think he'd go out with me?"

Her frank question took me by surprise. I didn't know Donna well enough to know if she was the type of girl Joseph went for. On the flip side, I didn't know Joseph well enough to know what kind of woman he desired. I would have liked to say he was into me, but as I checked Joseph's progress, he seemed more enrapt by the internal workings of my coffee machine than listening to two hormonal women swooning over him. "I have no idea, Donna. You'd have to ask him."

She apprehended my wrists as if we'd been best friends for years. "You think so? Oh, my gosh, I can't. What would I say to him? He'd probably say no anyway, wouldn't he?"

She was too busy casting quick covert glances toward

Joseph to notice my distress. The longer she held on to me, the more I felt my blood thickening in my veins. I pulled away and stepped back, forcing an amiable smile to hide my distaste.

The door of the café swung open, interrupting my ridiculous plot to fire her because of some mysteriously missing bills from the register. What can I say? I'm human. I turned away. "I'm going to check on a few things in my office. Call me if you need help," I said, gesturing toward the three new patrons.

I think Donna took the hint that I was not ready to be her BFF on such short notice. I walked past Joseph and around the corner to my small office, the sound of Donna's disappointment radiating from her practiced "Welcome to I Like You a Latte" greeting. It was a sweet song in my ears.

I dropped into my chair and studied the large calendar staring me down. Donna's name, written on every Saturday and Sunday square, jumped out at me, taunting me. Like the envious overlooked woman, I itched to take a bold Sharpie marker and black out her name in ebony scribbles. If that were not enough, I wanted to paint over the hideous, unforgiving scrawls with many layers of Wite-Out to hide my sinister jealousy.

I yanked open the middle drawer of the desk, just to check whether those weapons of choice were available to me, but slammed it shut before I did something foolish. I rolled my eyes and scolded myself for thinking such childish things. If anything, Donna could sue me for discrimination, if I'd removed her from the schedule without a viable reason. And she'd win. I'd lose everything over coveting a man who wasn't even mine to covet.

I drilled my palms into my eye sockets and shook off all thoughts of Donna and Joseph. Instead, I flipped the page of the calendar and set my sights on something more productive. I barely had time to go over next month's schedule when a tentative tapping brought my attention to the door. Joseph stood leaning against the frame, his arms crossed at his chest and a smug look on his face.

"You fixed it?"

I didn't mean to sound surprised. It wasn't that I didn't think Joseph *could* fix the espresso machine. I just didn't think he'd have the right tools for the job. Even as I sat there, I couldn't imagine one common thing between leaky barn roofs and broken coffee machines.

"Yeah, it was just a clogged water filter."

"And you had one of those in your trusty, rusty toolbox?"

He laughed aloud, loud enough for Donna and the rest of the place to hear. My heart soared.

"I actually found a spare in the cabinet below the

machine. I think the guy who was here the last time left you an extra on purpose, so he wouldn't have to miss another one of his daughter's soccer games to fix it."

"Smart man."

"No," Joseph amended, shutting the door. He strolled into my office and plopped his cute, little behind on the edge of my desk. "I'm the smart man who found it and installed it, even under the pressure of your employee's constant gaping. She really needs to learn the art of nonchalance."

Heat infused my cheeks. "I am so sorry. I'll say something to her."

Joseph waved it off. "Don't even worry about it. She's young. She's got the rest of her college years to smarten up." He clasped his hands together and grabbed his knee, hiking it up. His face scrunched in an odd sort of way. "Did you put her up to asking me out?"

My mouth fell open. "She asked you out?"

"Mm-hmm."

"Wow, she doesn't waste any time." I leaned back in my chair, inwardly wishing I had that kind of courage.

"Aren't you the least bit curious if I accepted?"

Curious didn't come close. Chomping at the bit was closer to what I felt, though a woman of my age would never give him the satisfaction. I picked up a pen, idly playing with it as I spoke. "Who you choose to date is your own business. Who am I to reprimand you for going out with a girl a decade younger than you?"

"So, you wouldn't approve."

"I didn't say that," I rectified. "I just think you need to remember that you don't have to rebound on every girl who comes along. You can have any woman of your choosing, and jumping into the dating scene again with a college girl who's barely over the legal drinking age is not one of your wiser decisions."

Joseph seemed to be enjoying himself, although I couldn't say I harvested much amusement from the matter.

"Don't worry. I let her down easy. I told her I was flattered with the offer, but I was too old for her. And that I had the hots for you."

The pen fell to the floor and my heart jumped in my throat. I had no way of knowing if he meant what he said or was just playing around. I dared him to come clean despite the meekness of my voice. "You didn't…"

He leaned across the desk, daring me back. "What if I did?"

I closed my eyes, imagining how difficult it now was going to be to work under the same roof with the girl. I heard the laughter in his voice and realized the joke was on me. I stiffened my chin. "No, really, what did you say to her?"

He stared at me for a moment, as if taking pleasure in my angst. "I told her that the guy who was checking her out as she filled his order was better suited for her."

"And she was okay with that?"

"Over the years, I've learned that desperate girls on the prowl have the attention span of gnats and will jump at anything that takes a second look at them. I bet if you asked Donna right now, she'd not be able to tell you my name, even though you introduced us. Now, you on the other hand, could probably list the number of men versus women patrons in the shop and what each is wearing."

"Is that so?" I asked, wondering if that was his idea of a compliment.

"Tell me I'm wrong," he stated, crossing his arms. "Better yet, I'd put money on the fact that you can tell me what I was wearing the first time we met."

The image of Joseph in a towel, bare-chested and delightfully muscled, came to mind. "Anyone who's not legally blind would remember what you were wearing. I don't think that counts."

"Fair enough. How about the second time we met?"

I sighed and looked toward the ceiling, drawing to mind that same evening when I came home from the grocery with my arms full. "You had on a tie and dress slacks. The tie was blue with navy stripes, the pants were khaki, and your shoes were shiny black like they were recently polished."

"See? I knew you're the type to take notice of these things."

"All right, smarty pants, what was I wearing?"

"Which time are we talking about?"

I crossed my arms, thinking he'd never get this right no matter which one I chose. Knowing he'd been too caught up in Caroline leaving him that one fateful morning, I decided on the most unlikely moment he'd recall his own hand in front of his face. "The first time we met."

Joseph pretended to think, scratching his head for theatrical purposes. "You were...not in a towel. Although that would have been nice to see."

My face probably flushed ten shades of red due to his charming little compliment. I bit my lip, hiding my absurd reaction over his flattery and waited for him to try again.

"You were dressed in jeans, winter boots trimmed in brown fur, a matching *Land's End* down parka, black leather gloves, and a red scarf. I'm going with handmade by your grandmother."

I stood in awe. My brow rose to heights beyond my hairline, if that were possible. I could not believe he rattled off what I had worn that day and with so much detail.

Simply put, he defied the laws of the virile man-code. "How in the world did you remember all that?"

"I shall not reveal my secrets," he said, hand over his heart. "Come on, let's get out of here."

Still stunned, I followed Joseph out of the office and noticed the warm smile on Donna's face as she locked eyes with him. He stealthily pointed toward a table of three men chatting it up about tonight's football game and gave a thumb's up. She mouthed "thank you" and shimmied around the counter to clean the nearest table and work her magic. Judging by the way she innocently tossed her long blond hair off her shoulder as she tidied up, I knew she'd have a lock on a future date before her shift ended. She was that good.

"You ready?" Joseph asked, handing me my coat and gloves. Another one of his irrepressible grins lit up his face. I then realized he was not the overly perceptive man he'd made himself out to be. I wore the same ensemble of winter apparel this morning as the first day we'd met.

I shook my head, feeling the fool. "You think you're so clever, don't you?"

"Hey, I remembered your red scarf, didn't I? You're not wearing that today. Surely, that should count for something?"

"I don't think so." I slipped my arms in the sleeves and

shrugged into my coat.

He put on his coat as well, but stopped to fasten mine. "Just answer me this," he said shooing my hands away and sliding the zipper up my midline. "Did your grandmother crochet your red scarf?"

Quoting him verbatim, I gave a satisfied smile. "I shall not reveal my secrets."

He tipped his head back in laughter. "She did and you know it."

Chapter Twelve

Riding with Joseph to his sister's house was the most fun I'd had in years. He talked on and on about his younger days and the typical, boyish trouble he'd gotten himself into on the family farm. From what I gathered, he had a memorable childhood filled with as many inexhaustible adventures as a curious country boy could find.

Now all grown up, I imagined the daring, exploratory lad had not left him completely. Just listening to the way he described the labyrinth of trails winding through his parents' woods, and the day he and his buddies built a tree house with his father's 'borrowed' tools they never returned, was proof he'd do it all over again.

I never had a family farm to while away my time on or a lake in the back forty to swim in on a hot July afternoon. We lived in the urban areas of Kentucky where the closest thing to a farm was Trauth Dairy in Newport.

As Joseph drove further south on I-75 and onto I-64, the panorama of fast food restaurants, gas stations, and franchised hotels drifted away. The view of concrete streets and traffic lights slowly faded into a scenic landscape of rolling meadows, black board fences, and fancy Thoroughbred horses.

From there, until we pulled into his sister's drive, I sat mesmerized by the beauty of the land. The trees had lost most of their leaves to the harsh approaching winds, but I could envision a paradise of red, orange, and gold blazing between lush green meadows and blue skies on picturesque autumn days.

Joseph dropped gears as we turned the bend and drove beneath a huge, rusty, wrought iron sign proudly welcoming me to *Pride & Joy Farm*. After descending a hill and turning another crook in the road, he slowed to a halt and killed the engine. For the first time since we left the expressway, I gazed at my handsome driver.

"This is where your sister lives?"

Joseph smiled as he took in the two-story farmhouse and the impressive tan and black barn with symmetrical gables in the distance. He released a long breath. "Yeah. This is it." He pointed beyond the barn to the outlying crop of hills and trees. "And that's my parents' place. On the other side of that is my other sister's farm, but she's not usually in town. She travels the States in search of rescue mustangs."

I took in the impressive scenery, combing the vast

estate with astonished eyes. "How could you leave such a grand place to live in downtown Cincinnati?"

"Caroline," he replied.

"What?" At first, I thought he called me by the wrong name.

He opened the door of his truck and shut it with a hard slam. As he walked around the front of the vehicle, I noticed the deep furrows in his brow. He opened my door for me and divulged the rest of the details. "Caroline had me move so I could be closer to her. She hated driving an hour and a half to see me. Said it was too far and inconvenient for her busy schedule. Like the sucker I am, I gave into her petty whims and thought it would be better for our relationship."

He let out a scoff, displaying his final take on the matter.

"I'm sorry, I shouldn't have pried."

"It's all right."

His truck was a large Ford diesel, so hopping out of the cab became more like BASE jumping. He steadied me as soon as my feet hit the blacktop. I tried to ignore the thrilling sensation of his strong hands grasping my arms, albeit covered by a thick down coat. But no way could I disregard the slightest touch given by Joseph. Every contact he made with me sent my heart skyrocketing toward the moon.

"I don't know about you, but I'm starving. That chronic temperamental espresso machine of yours depleted all my gumption for the day. Let's get some grub first," he suggested, "and then we can attack the barn full force."

I followed him up the sidewalk to the house and was floored when he didn't even knock. I wasn't used to the *mi casa es su casa* approach. My family was much more formal. We always called before visiting and knocked when we arrived.

He entered the home, as if he lived there, gave a shout for his sister, who didn't answer back, and continued his trek to the kitchen. Immediately, he opened the refrigerator door and began searching for something to eat. "What do you like? Turkey? Bologna? There's not much here. Look's like she's got some fried chicken…I could heat that up for us."

I suddenly felt like I was imposing. "I'm fine. I don't need to eat your sister's food."

His eyes landed hard on mine. "Don't hand me that crap. I know about your sugar issues. You're eating something and that's final. I'm not going to get you up on a barn roof, so you can pass out on me and plummet to your death. My sister would kill me."

"You're *giving* me a reason to kill you now, Joey?"

From behind the refrigerator door, a tall brunette in jeans, flannel shirt, and chaps walked into the kitchen. She resembled Joseph in many ways, but looked nothing like a man. She was all feminine—petite waist, small hands, and noticeable curves. But the unmistakable hardness in her eyes proved she was not a woman to mess with. I imagined she and Joseph often went round and round as children.

"Don't call me that," Joseph complained, shutting the fridge door. "You know I hate that name."

She glanced my way and smiled. I assumed the pleasant welcome was not for cordial reasons, but because she took pleasure in making her little brother squirm in front of a female guest.

"Well, Joseph, it's good to see you finally came to your senses and got rid of Caroline." She held out her hand, and when I accepted, she gripped it like a man and gave one hard pump. "I'm Candace. And you are?"

"Jamie," I offered. She seemed very delighted to meet me, although I think it stemmed from Joseph bringing someone else besides Caroline to her place.

"How long you two been dating?" Candace inquired, glancing between us.

For poor Joseph's sake, I felt compelled to speak right away. "Oh, we're not dating." I caught sight of him closing his eyes in embarrassment. "We're just friends."

Candace nodded, though she didn't look convinced. "Right."

Joseph cleared his throat and changed the subject. "I'm sorry my sister doesn't seem to have much to eat. As you can tell, she's got plenty to munch on with her big fat foot in her mouth."

Candace slapped the back of her brother's head and the unruly lock I'd grown fond of fell into his eye. "He's just bitter because he let a woman emasculate him, and he's yet to grow a pair after all these years."

"Unlike you who runs off every guy who's even remotely interested in you, with his tail tucked between his legs," Joseph added, raking his hair back into place.

"I can't help that I'm choosier than you." Candace shot me a quick apologetic look. "No offense."

I grinned at her. "None taken."

"Don't you have something to do?" Joseph pleaded earnestly.

I couldn't look at them with a straight face anymore. The sibling rivalry between them, even at their age, was beyond comical. I never had that with my sister because of our age difference. She moved out of the house before any kind of rivalry could exist.

"So, what did Joey bribe you with to get you to come out here?" Candace asked, leaning against the counter.

"He didn't bribe me with anything," I confessed, keeping a close eye on his reactions. "I wanted to come."

Joseph held my gaze as he crossed his arms. "I had to fix your espresso machine first before you accepted."

"Well," I said, biting my lip nervously. "Had it not needed fixing in the first place, I wouldn't have gotten the offer. I have a nasty bruise on my leg to prove it."

"Are you saying if I asked you to come with me, you would have?"

"Sure, why wouldn't I?"

We seemed to have forgotten about Candace being in the room, for neither of us could take our eyes off each other. I felt trapped in his gaze, the intensity of his private thoughts speaking volumes. I was not a mind reader, but I think I made the man happy by being here with him. My presence at his sister's farm, with no strings attached, seemed to mean more to him than anything I could have chosen to do with my day.

I wanted to let him know how much it meant for him to invite me, but something inside me told me it was better left unsaid. It was too soon to start divulging such emotions with Joseph, and I could imagine him tucking tail and running, just like Candace's boyfriends, the second I did.

"Okay..." Candace said, breaking up our quiet bonding moment. "I've got to get back to work. It was nice to meet you, Jamie." She patted me on the back as she crossed the kitchen. Before she exited, she shouted a warning over her shoulder. "Be careful on that roof today. It can be a slippery slope."

I wondered if her cautionary, cryptic words were for me, or if I was reading too much into them. I didn't have long to ponder. Joseph turned and dove into the refrigerator again. He reached in and selected the lunchmeat packages, cheese, and mayo.

"Bread's in the cabinet." He gestured toward the one behind me as he set the items on the counter.

I fetched the loaf, and together we made sandwiches. We didn't say much, but the occasional smiles and glances continued as we filled our stomachs. About half an hour later, we made our way to the barn.

The journey to the building was longer than I expected. From his truck, everything looked extraordinary, and I suppose actual distances didn't register then. My eyes remained on the ground, and eventually our pace fell into step with each other's. I felt like the band members from the iconic sixties slapstick comedy TV show, *The Monkees*, though our arms were not intertwined. Joseph realized our synchronized stride as well and gave a little chuckle.

Despite the smile on his face, he looked as though he was plagued with heavy thoughts.

"Are you all right?" I asked, shielding my eyes from the glaring sun as I looked up at him.

"Yeah," he played off. "I'm fine. But I should probably apologize for my sister. She's kind of a hard nose and forgets that some of us have feelings. I hope she didn't make you feel uncomfortable."

"No, not at all. She's funny actually."

Joseph's brow rose. "You're joking, right?"

"Look, you don't have to coddle me because your sister brought up Caroline. I know she was a big part of your life, and, whether your family agreed with that relationship or not, she was your friend. I get that. I hope you realize I'm not trying to step into her place by being with you."

"Your shoes are too big anyway."

"What?" I looked down at my size six feet. "Caroline's feet are smaller than mine? That's impossible. She's almost as tall as you."

Joseph averted his eyes and searched the open sky. "Don't be so literal, Jamie. That's not what I meant."

"What did you mean then?"

Joseph stopped walking and blocked my forward motion with his arm. He turned his entire body to face me, hands on his hips. He took a deep breath and held it, words failing him. The color of the bright, cerulean sky behind him was no match for the vivid swirls of blue dancing in his eyes. They nearly entranced me as he stood there fighting the urge to express his mind.

I saw his Adam's apple bob, and I almost believed he was about to say 'never mind.' Then he took another long breath of courage and spoke. "If Caroline tried to stand in your shoes, Jamie, she would fail to fill them. You are so much bigger than she could hope to be. And I'm not talking bone structure here. I'm talking about good old-fashioned charisma, character, and kindness. You have all those qualities and more, and not because you're trying. It's just the way you are…what's inside you."

He glanced at his feet, giving me a small moment of reprieve from his dazzling eyes. I couldn't begin to predict the next words that would fall from his lips or the sight of welled-up tears threatening to fall when he looked back up at me. My heart melted to see such emotion in Joseph. I treasured it. But honestly, I had no idea how to deal with the sudden outpouring.

"I didn't know I needed someone like you," he began slowly, "until you showed up. I was perfectly fine being me. The playboy without a heart. Caroline's accused me so many times of not having one, I began to think she was right. Then you came along, and…"

"And?"

His voice grew quiet. "And…something stirred inside me. When I saw you that morning, in the hall, you made me forget all about the darkness in my world. And trust me," he whispered, striking his chest with a fist, "there's so much in here…you don't even know."

I watched as he came to terms with himself for sharing that little bit of information. He looked as if he were trying to convince himself that I could be trusted with the rest of his innermost feelings. I wanted to assure him that he could. Under normal circumstances, despite my diminutive physique, I could be a solid rock upon which to stand. But honestly, the ground beneath my own feet was shifting, and I couldn't gain a firm stance for myself, let alone Joseph.

He shuffled his boots on the pavement. "You probably wouldn't understand, but lately I've had a hard time. I've been in a fog, and I can't seem to find the joy in life. I-I've just been running on autopilot. You know, the-world-must-go-on kind of mentality. And then I met you."

He laughed at himself, as if he couldn't believe what was coming out of him. "Short of sounding like a cheesy, hopeless romantic…you were like a ray of sunshine. And for the first time in a long time, I actually felt the warmth of someone's smile. Your smile."

He fidgeted some more. "I don't wanna lose that feeling. And I certainly don't want to lose you." He hung his head and stroked the heart tattoo on his wrist. "Like everyone else I ever cared about."

Chapter Thirteen

I trembled like the lone leaf on a tree, enduring the brunt force of Joseph's words. At any moment, depending on the might of the next gust, I felt like I would be bowled over and swept away. My mind had already gotten caught up in the whirlwind. The chaotic circulation of my thoughts was too random for my brain to select just one and process it. If I tried to speak, I knew I'd only end up looking the fool.

Joseph continued to stare at his wrist, tracing the script-like initials inked on his skin. I had never suffered the loss of a sibling, or anyone in my immediate family, so I had no inkling of what he was going through or what I could say to comfort him. All I knew was I hated this awkward silence.

I was certain this wasn't the first time he'd dealt with someone being uncomfortable in this situation. I imagined he had gotten that a lot at the funeral. But the last thing I wanted to be was the typical individual who tried to smooth things over with misguided words and impersonal encouragement.

I reached out and touched his hand. His skin was warm against mine. He lifted his eyes to me, the pain and weariness of his long-term grief etched in the tiny lines around them. I prepared to say something—what exactly I had no idea—but he dropped his arms to his side and retreated from my touch.

"Can you give me a sec?"

I had no time to answer. He had already removed himself from the piss-poor effort on my part and made a beeline for his truck parked in front of the house. He had plenty of time to gather his wits and shake off the blues. When he returned with his toolbox, he feigned a smile.

"Before you say anything," he said, squeezing his eyes shut and sighing. "I just want to say I don't tell everyone about...this. I just...I want you to know I'm telling you the truth."

"I know that, Joseph," I agreed, rocking back on my heels. "You've always spoke the truth, and that's one of the many things I like about you. I'm glad you felt comfortable enough to share your feelings with me. I'm honored, and you can rest assured that it's safely tucked away in here."

After patting my chest, I clutched my trembling hands together. I had more to say and needed to find a way to speak as forthcoming as Joseph had. I brought to mind the courage he had found moments before he escaped to his truck and seized the proverbial bull by the horns. "You're not going to lose me, Joseph. No matter what happens, I'll never stop being your friend."

This time, the smile that lighted his face was sincere and genuine. I'd brought joy to him with a few simple words, words I meant and would uphold. He needed me. Strangely enough, I needed him too. Like him, I didn't know it until we met.

Life had a funny way of reminding a person of what was needed. I thought I was the self-sufficient woman and coffee-house owner who didn't need a shoulder to lean on. I had gained all I had without the help of anyone. What I didn't realize until now was that the fruits of my labor were all for nothing.

What good were a successful business, a growing bank account, and a promising future if I had no one to share it with? I wasn't thinking about marriage or a committed lovers' relationship. I was ruminating over the importance of companionship and an honest camaraderie with someone I could trust.

I'd never before felt this way about any man. To me, men were nothing but lying, cheating, unreliable SOBs who sucked us in with their charm, weaseled their way into our hearts, and tore it out of our chest at a moment's notice with no regret.

Joseph was not like that. Sure, I'd said that about several hopeful suitors in my past, but this time I knew differently. He was a man who knew what it meant to be forsaken. He knew what it felt like to be helplessly sunk in bottomless sorrow. He knew the pain of loss and grief and would never put someone else through the same anguish. No matter what Caroline had claimed, Joseph had the biggest heart of any man I'd ever known.

My beliefs about Joseph were immediately confirmed the second he dropped his toolbox to the ground and wrapped me in his strong arms. The strength of his solid embrace knocked the wind from my lungs. I saw stars, fireworks, and lightening streaks behind my eyelids. My heart pounded against the boom of my bubbling emotions. I had imagined so many times what his hugs would feel like, yet the real thing was so much more. It was safe. A sanctuary. Heaven.

I relished this wonderful moment, taking in every splendid sensation of his hand climbing up the back of my neck and splaying into my hair as he pulled me tighter against him. His fingertips gently cradled my head and I took a deep breath, memorizing his intoxicatingly masculine scent. Though blanketed with a thick winter coat, the heady aroma of his warm skin permeated around me.

Thick Carhartt canvas never smelled so good.

Tentatively, Joseph released me. His face was alight with happiness and appreciation. Together, we overcame a huge obstacle, and it seemed we were no worse for wear.

He cleared his throat and clasped his hands together. "Okay," he muttered, taking another step back.

Amazingly, I was grateful for the space as much as he. Had he held me any longer, I might have sequestered him from his duties and stowed him away from the rest of the world with no remorse.

I was so screwed. I had promised myself I'd never fall for another man ever again and here I was considering the idea of handing myself to Joseph on a platter.

"As much as I hate to say this," he pointed over his shoulder, "that barn is screaming my name."

"Right. I hear it too. Or maybe it's Candace," I searched for her in the fields, "groaning in agony from our little public display of affection."

Joseph glanced around the farm with a devious grin. "I don't care. Let her groan. She'll get over it. Besides," he said, cocking his head to the side. "I think she'd like you to stick around."

"You think?"

Joseph blew out a sardonic breath and bent to retrieve his toolbox. "Trust me, if she didn't want you around me, you'd know it. There's one thing about Candace, she's more honest than I am."

"Should I take that as a fair warning?"

His hearty laughter carried in the breeze, whisking through my hair. "Oh, yeah."

Chapter Fourteen

In the course of a few hours, I learned many important life lessons. Don't look down once atop a two-story barn roof. Don't assume the gutter will catch anything other than rain. (We lost many screws to this principle—or to be more precise, I lost them.) And don't forget that cordless drills slide down a six-twelve pitch metal roof rather quickly.

What I had put Joseph through today, would have made the typical man blow a gasket. A two-hour job ended up taking twice as long because I was not accustomed to manual labor twenty feet in the air. Joseph didn't seem to mind. In fact, it was the most I'd ever heard him laugh.

Don't get me wrong. I received my share of I-can't-believe-you-just-did-that kind of cringes from him, especially when I accidentally bumped the ladder with my foot and it slid sideways down the face of the gutter until it crashed to the ground. However, I was fortunate that Joseph had a soft spot for my expression of apologetic desperation. "Timmm-ber" was my timid attempt to make light of the hefty mistake.

Once we replaced the old ring-shank nails with modern rubber washers and hex-head screws, and Candace came to rescue us from our lofty prison on the tin roof, Joseph whisked me away into the thick of his family's pine tree forest. We followed a narrow dirt path, which Joseph explained was a worn deer path, until it opened up to a recently-plowed hay field and a massive crystalline lake sparkling in the sunlight.

We walked its perimeter for a while, discussing the things we enjoyed most as kids. My stories were not as interesting as Joseph's, and I found myself enthralled with his memories of the days on this very lake.

"So, your parents used to own this part of the farm too?"

"It was one huge plantation until they divvied up parcels for each of us kids. When I moved to Cinci, I sold my piece of property to my sister, Miranda, the one who rescues wild mustangs. Dad wasn't all that happy about it, since I was his only son, but she needed it more than I did. At least, I kept it in the family. Anyway, this lake was my favorite place as a kid. If I still owned my land, it would butt up against Candace's on the west side."

I looked out over the water and watched the dried-up cattails sway in the breeze. I pitied Joseph that he'd given up his piece of heaven for someone as unworthy as Caroline. The more I found out about her, the more I resented what she'd done to him. He didn't deserve it, and she definitely didn't deserve his loyal friendship. If wishes could come true, I'd wished he had never met her.

As much as I could muster, I pushed away my dark thoughts of Caroline and returned to Joseph's lovely haven he chose to share with me. "I can see why you liked this place so much."

Joseph found my hand and dragged me down toward the east side of the lake. "Come on. I want to show you something."

I ran with him, having no idea what could be so important. The cool wind rushed past me in our exuberant jog, but all I could feel was the warmth of Joseph's grasp. The thrill of his enthusiasm radiated through me, and I realized at that very moment how much I appreciated the strength of a working man's hands.

I had never dated a guy who made an honest living from manual labor. Most of the men I attracted were paper-pushers, IT guys, or lazy I'll-just-let-you-bring-home-the-bacon losers. There was much to be said about the responsible men of this decade who still aspired to support themselves by the sweat of their brow and not by the handouts of a sucker girlfriend.

As I continued to savor the feel of Joseph's calloused hand, we finally stopped at the base of an age-old tree at the edge of the lake. Its trunk was about as wide as I was tall with rungs of weathered wood planks nailed up its face. Joseph looked up and reached for the lowest branch.

"Come on," he urged, bracing his foot on the first step. He hoisted himself onto the limb and continued to climb.

I glanced up at the dizzying height of the tree and saw the decrepit, makeshift, childhood tree house balanced on a limb three branches up. "You've got to be kidding. I can't get up there."

Joseph glanced down after he successfully secured himself in the V of the next bough. "Sure you can. If you can hang out on a twenty-foot high barn roof, you can climb a tree."

"There's a difference," I said, crossing my arms in defiance.

"How so?"

"The surface area of a roof, no matter how high, is considerably larger than the bottom-most branch of this tree. You do remember the many things that fell from the roof, don't you? If you haven't realized, I'm a bit of a klutz." I shifted the weight of my body on my other foot for emphasis. "No way am I getting up there."

Joseph outstretched his hand to me. "I won't let you fall. Promise."

The pledge he made, on top of the sincerity in his voice that he wouldn't let me descend to my demise, had me agreeing to this ridiculous feat in less than a flash. Although my skittish heart pounded in my chest, I huffed away my fears in one hasty sigh and prepared to make my ascent.

"Grab hold of that limb with your right hand," Joseph instructed, "and put your left foot on the rung. At the count of three, you're going to push up and grab my forearm."

I gave him one last look of trepidation, hoping he'd say to forget it. Evidently, I didn't sell it well enough. "Trust me" was his response.

Putting all my faith in Joseph's powerful grip and his strapping body wedged in the fork of the tree, I counted aloud and reached as high as I could for his arm on 'three.' He groaned and growled as he tugged me higher.

"Use your feet," he gritted through his clenched jaw, his face turning red.

As he ordered, I stepped from plank to plank until I reached the height of his chest.

"The limb beside you. Use it," he said in a labored, breathless voice. Taking hold of the branch allowed for the dead weight of my body to release the strain on his. We had further to go, but at least I stood atop the first branch.

"You okay?" he asked, panting.

Still shaking like a leaf, I nodded an affirmative.

"The next part is easier since the limbs are closer," he reassured. "You just have to reach and hold tight to me, once I lug you across. Balance is everything, got it?"

Balance. Right. I wanted to laugh. If he knew the catastrophe I had caused in ballet school when I was ten, he wouldn't be risking his life just to get me into a warped, childhood camp that had seen better days.

"Are you sure it's safe?" I asked, clutching the trunk with the fervor of a stubborn two-year old and her security blanket.

"You can do this." He patted my tensed arm and tilted his head in the most adoring fashion. That cursed lock of hair fell across his brow, and I was smitten. "Just lunge for me, and I'll catch you."

Under the direction of Joseph's practiced tree-climbing skills, I did exactly as he said and sprang from my limb to his. My arms snaked around his torso like a boa constrictor, and I screamed as we teetered together in a tight embrace. I saw the ground, who knows how many feet down, and shut my eyes.

I felt one powerful arm across my back, and I assumed

he had his other anchored firmly around the girth of the trunk. After a few more grunts from the male chest into which I had resorted to burying my face, the struggle to stay on the limb ceased. I slowly opened my eyes and peeled my cheeks off the safety of his coat.

Joseph looked at me with pride, his face smeared with a handsome roguish grin. "Piece of cake."

With my heart in my throat, I attempted to ascertain the height of my idiotic upward hike, but Joseph stopped me. His palm cupped my jaw in the most delicate manner, as if the bones of my face would break under his touch.

"Don't look down," he whispered. "Just keep your eyes on me."

Awestruck by the indigo ring encircling the light fissures of blue irises, I was incapable of looking elsewhere. Long, midnight lashes fell on high cheekbones as his gaze lowered over my mouth. I absorbed the beauty of his face, his full, sensual lips outlined by a manly shadow of scruff. His mouth was the perfect medium for kissing.

Pressed against him, I swore I could feel the beating of his heart through the padding of our coats. I wondered if he could feel mine. I felt lightheaded, lethargic in his embrace as I waited for his next move.

Joseph let out a huge breath and withdrew his head. His arms loosened around me, and I felt the tenseness of his muscles relax. "We're almost there."

I blinked rapidly, trying to shake away the fog of our near-kiss moment. Disappointment racked my whole body, but I pulled as much contentment as I could from somewhere deep in my soul.

I tore my eyes away from his gorgeous face and geared myself up for the next hike up the tree to the nearby platform, sided with battered wood slats and a hanging rope ladder. The wind whipped against us at this height, but I felt hot and sweaty. I tugged at the zipped-up collar of my parka, overheating in its downy sheath.

"Go ahead," Joseph ushered, holding out his arm to steady me as I snagged the line dangling from the limb above my head. "I got you."

Reminding myself not to look down, I climbed the last steps to our destination with Joseph quickly following behind me. Frightened about the wood floor giving way beneath my weight, I waited for him to give me the go-ahead.

Sifting past me, he stepped out and seized the rickety railing. His eyes searched the distant horizon. I assumed he was letting it all come back to him—the memories, the emotions, the nostalgia. He glanced over his shoulder and extended his hand. "Care to join me?"

I put my hand in his and allowed him to lead me

forward. I took in the breathtaking view of a colorful sunset hovering over pillows of far-off rolling hills. The lake mirrored a sheet of glass, reflecting the setting sun in its soft ripples. The treetops stood at attention, saluting a fine ending to another blissful day in their existence. I forgot all about the disenchantment I'd felt removing myself from Joseph's arms moments ago.

I looked at Joseph. The profile of his sharply chiseled face boasted one more added bonus amid the stunning picture. Feeling the weight of my stare, he looked at me. His smile beamed brighter than any noonday sun.

I drew in a huge breath, taking in the clean country air.

"This," he claimed proudly, "was where I spent most of my boyhood days. I used to pretend the treehouse was a pirate ship, sailing over tumultuous seas in search of buried treasure and bonny lasses."

A wave of courage rushed through me as I contemplated the nostalgic place to which Joseph brought me. "Did you bring any of your dates aboard?"

He chuckled and shook his head. "Nope. You're the first girl who's ever been up here."

"Caroline didn't chase you up this tree?"

He looked at me askance, as if I should know better. "I couldn't get her up here, if I'd paid her." He drifted back in thought. "I take that back. My sister came up here once.

But only once."

"Candace?"

He shook his head.

I tried again. "Miranda?"

His eyes fell to his wrist. "Lindsey."

I reached out and gingerly touched his tattoo. "Are these her initials?" Technically, I knew the answer since I'd overheard his conversation with Caroline about her in the hall, but I played dumb.

He smiled and gave a tender nod of his head.

I suddenly recanted my castle-in-the-sky type wish about Caroline and decided it would be better to cast one in favor of sparing Joseph the loss of his sister.

"She was dating the high school jock, and, to impress him, she brought him here. She told me secretly that she wanted to win his heart by showing him that she was worthy of his affections. Between you and me, though," he sneered, "the guy was an ass."

I couldn't help but laugh with him. I watched him closely as he continued the story of his beloved sister.

"She got him to climb the tree and dared him to swing from that rope." He pointed to the thick-knotted strand of boat line hanging a few limbs up. My heart fell like a stone as I imagined when Joseph had climbed higher to secure it back in the day.

"Did he take the dare?"

"Like the typical beefcake who had more muscle than guts, he made up all kinds of excuses not to. Said he was putting his professional football career on the line and his coach would kill him."

The laugh lines in his face grew deeper as he told the rest.

"Lindsey finally realized he wasn't all that and a bag of chips and left his sorry ass in the tree house. She commandeered the rope and swung out. She even finished with a perfect dive just for kicks. She and I swam the rest of the afternoon while Mr. Wannabee Brett Favre spent his day trying to figure out how to get out of the tree without falling and breaking his neck."

A bout of companionable silence overtook us. While Joseph probably used the moments to reminisce about his time with his deceased sister, I exhausted mine wondering how I could get him to tell me more about her.

Finally, I caved. "You don't speak of her much, do you?"

"Not if I don't have to." He idly spread a pile of leaves around with his boot. "It's hard for me to open up about stuff like that. It hurts to think about how she died."

I covered his hand with mine. "I don't need to know that stuff. I would never want you to have to relive that day over anyway. But..." I said, dragging out the word long enough for me to get my thoughts in line. "I'd love to hear about her. Only when you're ready though, Joseph. We have time."

He turned and captured me with a look I hadn't expected. His eyes pierced through me and tethered my heart to the hope of knowing all there was to know about his life, past and present.

He gestured toward the wood floor of the tree house and lowered himself in a cross-legged position. "Sit down. I'll tell you all about her."

I sat across from him, elated beyond words that he was about to let somebody in on his treasured memories—and that someone was me.

He inched closer and took my hand as he spoke. "There was this one time when Lindsey came to see me when the band play at Bogart's. The place was packed, and she shows up right when..."

Chapter Fifteen

I stood in the hallway of my apartment complex, struggling to unlock my door. I had spent the entire day with an amazing man and was not looking forward to saying goodbye. When I woke up this morning, I had no idea I would fix a barn roof, climb a hundred-year-old tree, and watch the sun go down from the observation deck of an imaginary pirate ship. Joseph had breathed more life in me today than I'd ever drawn in during the course of my nonexistent life, and he made me laugh more than any clown who'd hit the Barnum and Bailey circuit.

My hands trembled as I fumbled with the few keys I had left on the ring. I then realized it was not the amount of keys that had kept me from inserting it into the slot, but Joseph. From the moment I met him, he made such an impression that I seemed to lose all hand-eye coordination.

"Here," Joseph offered, setting his toolbox down and taking over the task. "Let me help you." With deft hands, he slid the key into the lock, turned, and shoved the door open. He dangled the keys above my hand and dropped them into my palm with cool casualness. "There you go."

"Thanks."

I rocked on my heels, squeezing the jagged metal in my grasp. *Say something,* I demanded of myself.

"We still on for Friday?' Joseph asked, as if he possessed telepathic abilities.

"Friday?" I could barely get a grip on today, let alone try to recall plans five days from now.

He seemed to enjoy my sudden onset of dementia and jabbed his thumbs in his jean pockets. "Yesterday you accepted my offer to take you out this weekend. Changing your mind? 'Cause it's okay, if you are. I won't hold it against you."

The events of the weekend all rushed back to me. "I'm not changing my mind. I look forward to our date." As soon as I heard the term come out of my mouth, I backpedaled. "I mean…our evening together as friends."

"You don't have to dance around the word. I don't mind, if you call it a date. It is what it is. Some might even call today a date. Like your detail-greedy friend, Melissa, for instance."

I had to agree. Melissa would so call this a date, especially once she found out about the near-kiss moment in the tree house. "I guess we can't dodge that bullet, can we?"

He leaned against the wall and braced his arm on the doorframe. "Only if we tried. But I'm not so eager to move out of the way. Call me a thrill seeker."

I reckoned I'd be one too, if the thrill ride included Joseph in the seat next to me. I tucked a loose strand of hair behind my ear, trying to collect one ounce of bravado. All day, we never ceased to run out of conversation, but now when it mattered most, I couldn't come up with a single word to say to this guy.

I wanted to tell him how grateful I was he'd invited me to his sister's farm and taught me how to reinforce roof slats under a tin covering without replacing the whole thing. I wanted to thank him for sharing his precious memories of Lindsey with me. I wanted to praise him for assisting me out of the tree house without letting me fall to my death. I wanted to let him know how thoughtful he was to run through the drive-thru on the way home, making sure my sugar levels were up. I wanted to admit how much it meant to me just to be near him. But I couldn't verbalize any of those thoughts into sensible sentences, if my life depended on it.

All my life I've always been the one to ruin a good thing in the start of a relationship. Too many times I said things that I thought were considerate and somehow I gave the impression I was ready to plan a wedding. Guys freak out when you say things like "I had a really nice time. We should do this again" or "That was so sweet of you of you to think of me. You're definitely a keeper." Chickens.

So, yeah, it was my turn to be a chicken now. This was the beginning stages of something too good to be true, and I wasn't about to mess it up with stupid words of appreciation. He'd have to come out and ask me if I enjoyed myself before I'd ever burst that dam.

Joseph dropped the casual façade and pushed off the wall, stepping toward me. Out of instinct, I drew back. The opposite side of the doorframe halted my retreat and my keys clinked against the wood as my hands coupled behind me, bracing myself for his approach.

"I had a wonderful time today," he declared, his body inches from mine.

"Me too," I squeaked before I could clear my throat.

"Would you go back, if I asked you again?"

I tried to pretend the close proximity of his muscled body, even hidden behind a winter coat, didn't bother me. "Do I have to sabotage something at the coffee shop before you'll extend the invitation?"

He faked giving it thorough consideration. "I don't think that's necessary."

"Good." I heaved a fake sigh of relief. "It could get pretty costly for me otherwise."

Joseph ignored my joke and brought his hand up to my face, brushing the back of his fingertips against my cheek. His eyes traced a course across the contours of my brow, down the crooked edge of my nose, and over the curves of my lips.

"You'll have to forgive me, Jamie."

He slid his hand along the slant of my jaw and closed the distance between us with a final momentous step. His head dipped and the tip of his nose grazed mine.

I felt his warm breath skim across my skin. "F-forgive you for what?"

His eyelids lowered with shameless desire and the stringent muscle in his jaw clenched. "For wanting to do this all day."

By the time his confession fell from his lips, he had taken mine in a light, sensual kiss. His mouth pressed tenderly upon my upper lip while the prickle of his scruffy face tickled my chin. His lips were, by far, the softest I had ever felt, warm satiny flesh wreaking havoc on my pathetic, athirst body. I'd waited so long—yearned for a man as perfect as Joseph. Were we moving too fast?

He pulled me closer, wrapping his other arm around my back, securing me in the strength of his mighty embrace. His tongue caressed the sensitive plateau of my bottom lip, testing me, teasing me.

He tasted of sweet menthol from the lingering flavor of mints he'd offered on the way home. I then realized he had planned this all along, and I forgave him of the offense. Admittedly, I was guilty of the same.

As abruptly as the kiss began, he ended it, stepping out my arms before I was ready. Still shaking from the wonders of everything that made Joseph the man he was, I stared at him for what seemed like forever. And he let me.

"What was that for?" I asked, feeling my knees buckle.

"I'm just doing what my fortune told me to do." He pulled his wallet from his back pocket and slipped a tiny rectangular piece of paper from behind his credit card. Taking hold of my hand, he pressed it into my palm and closed my fingers over it. He brought my hands together, and raised them up to his lips. He pressed a long, blissful kiss on my knuckles and backed away.

"Goodnight, Jamie," he said, picking up the toolbox at his feet. With another devilish smile, he winked and strolled down the hall to his apartment door. "See you Friday."

As soon as his door closed behind him, I opened my hand and saw he had left me a fortune reading from a cookie with yesterday's date scribbled on the bottom. Thinking back, I had vaguely remembered him snatching a cookie from the table and tucking it into his pocket before he left. Our conversation filtered into my memory...

"What's it say?"

He shook his head. "It's my fortune, not yours."

"That's not fair."

"Some other time, maybe," he said, tucking it into his jeans pocket. "You need to sleep."

Realizing that Joseph had given me a chance to read the prediction he'd acquired the day before, I promptly flipped it over and read what was written.

At this very moment you can change the rest of your life.

I gasped, my eyes lifting to the distant door down the hallway. Joseph's door. The door to the most unpredictable, charming, and generous man I'd ever had the privilege to meet.

Coiling my fingers around the sentimental paper, I held fast to the anticipation of Friday evening, wondering what other fates we might embark upon. As I stepped into my apartment, something unusual happened—an optimistic thought entered my mind.

This could be the start of something good.

THE END

Author's Note

The names of my fun-loving protagonists, Jamett and Joseph, came from the reminiscence of my imaginary friends when I was a little girl. While I no longer indulge in invisible camaraderie, their names stayed with me into adulthood.

With this in mind, I wanted to take my childhood friends and recreate them into something more profound than a distant memory of my tender youth. I wanted to build a believable world where two unlikely people grew to be steadfast friends and eventually fell in love despite the odds. I thank you for reading the first book of the *Jamett and Joseph* series, and I encourage you to continue with the sequels:

The Road to Something Better
The Gift of Something Grand

If you enjoyed this book by Renee Vincent, please consider leaving an honest review at your favorite vendor. Reviews not only give credibility to an author's work, they also help other readers find quality books worth reading.

About Renee Vincent

RENEE VINCENT is a *USA Today* bestselling author of romance and women's fiction. Her books have earned numerous accolades, including a #1 Bestseller for Viking Romance.

She lives on a secluded hundred-acre horse farm in the rolling hills of Kentucky with her husband, two beautiful daughters, a couple of nocturnal dogs, and a pair of cats who think they're the masters of the house. Truth be told…they are.

www.ReneeVincent.com

Books By Series

Vikings of Honor Series
Sunset Fire, Book 1
Emerald Glory, Book 2
Souls Reborn, Book 3
Tempered Steel, Book 4

Mavericks of Meeteetse Series
Longing for Langston, Brody & Liv, Book 1
Made for McKinley, Jonas & Ava, Book 2
Falling For Forester, Cole & Crys, Book 3
Wild for Wallace, Sawyer & Charlotte, Book 4

Jamett & Joseph Series
The Start of Something Good, Book 1
The Road to Something Better, Book 2
The Gift of Something Grand, Book 3

Stand Alone Novel
Silent Partner

Mailing List

Sign up for Renee Vincent's author newsletter and reap the benefits of being one of her loyal subscribers! One lucky winner is drawn each month. What's more, you get a FREE BOOK just for joining.

Go to ReneeVincent.com, then click on "Newsletter" to sign up and start reading!

ReneeVincent.com